"Can you raise y

She did that, feeling s
dress. From the wedd
run away from it...

"Okay, very carefully, I want you to try to move your
head—can you do that?"

She could do that, too.

"Any pain with that? Any tingling in your shoulders, arms
or legs?"

"No."

"Nothing? No pain—shooting or otherwise?" the man
asked.

"No," she said softly as she went on assessing his face
and finding more and more to it that made him seem like
the boy she'd known. And loved.

And learned to wish she hadn't...

Those full lips.

Those eyebrows that were a little thick and as dark a
brown as his hair.

Then her neck was free and he raised his eyes to her face.

And that was when she knew for sure.

No one except the Madison brothers and their sister,
Kinsey, had eyes like that. Cobalt blue that was bluer than
blue.

"Oh, my God!" she said in alarm.

"What? Pain? Numbness?" he asked with more urgency.

"You're Conor Madison," she accused scornfully.

He relaxed and nodded. "Hi, Maicy," he said calmly.

"I get it—I've died and gone to hell," she muttered.

CAMDEN FAMILY SECRETS:
Finding family and love in Colorado!

Dear Reader,

Maicy Clark is a runaway bride in a blizzard when she swerves to avoid hitting a deer on a mountain road. The next thing she knows, she's in a log cabin looking up into her rescuer's too-handsome face. The too-handsome face that belongs to her first love and the guy who hugely disappointed her when she was seventeen.

Navy doctor Conor Madison has a very full plate even before he comes across an unconscious woman in a snowstorm. The fact that that woman turns out to be his biggest regret, and that he's stranded with her while there's somewhere else he desperately needs to be, only makes matters worse.

So what happens when these two are isolated together with no one to depend on but each other and a whole lot of time to sort through old wounds? Let's just say that the wood in the fireplace isn't the only thing that's combustible.

Happy reading!

Victoria Pade

AWOL Bride

—

Victoria Pade

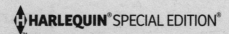

HARLEQUIN® SPECIAL EDITION®

Recycling programs
for this product may
not exist in your area.

ISBN-13: 978-0-373-62367-9

AWOL Bride

Copyright © 2017 by Victoria Pade

Printed in U.S.A.

Victoria Pade is a *USA TODAY* bestselling author of numerous romance novels. She has two beautiful and talented daughters—Cori and Erin—and is a native of Colorado, where she lives and writes. A devoted chocolate lover, she's in search of the perfect chocolate-chip-cookie recipe.

For information about her latest and upcoming releases, visit Victoria Pade on Facebook—she would love to hear from you.

Books by Victoria Pade

Harlequin Special Edition

Camden Family Secrets

The Marine Makes His Match

The Camdens of Colorado

A Camden's Baby Secret
Abby, Get Your Groom!
A Sweetheart for the Single Dad
Her Baby and Her Beau
To Catch a Camden
A Camden Family Wedding
It's a Boy!
A Baby in the Bargain
Corner-Office Courtship

Montana Mavericks: Rust Creek Cowboys

The Maverick's Christmas Baby

Montana Mavericks: Striking It Rich

A Family for the Holidays

Visit the Author Profile page
at Harlequin.com for more titles.

Chapter One

"This is not turning into a good time."

There was no one else in the rented SUV to hear Conor Madison's observation as he drove through a Montana snowstorm that was getting worse by the minute.

When his plane had landed in Billings on that mid-January Sunday, snow had been falling. As promised, he'd called his sister Kinsey to tell her he'd arrived safely. But when he did, he'd discovered that Kinsey wasn't in their small hometown of Northbridge, where she and Conor were slated to meet. Instead, she was snowed in inside her Denver home.

And by now, the snow was in his path, piling up fast. Conor could barely see two feet in front of him on this mountain road.

And on top of that, he was worried about his brother and thinking this whole idea might have been a mistake.

When he'd left the veterans' hospital in Maryland, his younger brother Declan's condition had been stable. In fact, Declan—who had been severely wounded in Afghanistan—had been doing so well he'd pushed Conor to make this trip. But when Conor had talked to Declan from the Billings airport, Declan hadn't sounded very well, though he'd insisted that Conor stay.

But an hour and a half into the drive, when he'd called to check in with Declan again, Declan had been even more sluggish and lethargic, and had informed Conor that he'd spiked a fever—which could herald a dangerous complication that Conor wouldn't be there to monitor.

As a doctor Conor couldn't treat family, but he could follow what was being done closely. Monitoring his brother's condition was the reason he was on leave from his own duties from the navy. Now he wasn't where he felt he should be—by his brother's side. If he hadn't learned that all flights in and out had been canceled due to the storm, he might have headed back.

But there was no going back either to Billings or to Maryland, so all Conor could do was get somewhere safe—and get back to worrying about his brother once he arrived.

He'd grown up around here so he recognized where he was—about fifteen miles outside of Northbridge. But visibility was getting worse by the minute, and he was having more and more trouble plowing through the deepest of the drifts. There was no way he was going to make those last fifteen miles.

Luckily he wasn't far from a cabin owned by the family of an old friend. When he noticed his patchy cell service was working for the moment, he'd called

Rickie Dale to find out if the cabin was still standing and if he could use it.

Thankfully, the answer to both of those questions had been yes.

Just before he reached the turnoff, he saw the first car he'd seen in the last hour—nose-first in a ditch.

The sedan's horn was blaring and the driver's side door was ajar so the dome light was on. In the dim glow he could see that the driver was still in the car, slumped over the steering wheel.

As a doctor, his duty was clear. He came to a slippery stop and ran against the wind to the other vehicle.

The driver was a woman. In a sleeveless wedding dress without so much as a coat on over it. There was an abundance of blood from a head wound, likely the result of hitting the windshield since—for some unknown reason—the airbag hadn't activated.

She didn't react to him opening her door. He couldn't even tell if she was breathing. So the first thing he did was check for a pulse, grateful to note that it was strong. She might be unconscious, but she was alive.

"Miss!" he shouted to be heard over the howling wind. "Can you hear me?"

She didn't so much as moan.

But Conor was a doctor of emergency and trauma medicine and a commander in the United States Navy, trained to work in the field. He knew what to do.

He took off his jacket and wrapped it firmly around her neck to stabilize it. Then, keeping her head and neck aligned, he eased her back against the seat.

She had a massive amount of hair and much of it had fallen forward into her face, heavily coated in blood.

Still, something about her struck him as familiar. But nothing concrete clicked for him, with his focus on her condition. Right now, all that mattered was getting her out of this cold.

He dashed back to his SUV and opened the passenger door, lowering that seat so it was as flat as it would go. Then he ran back to the sedan. With special care to keep her head and neck supported, he eased her from behind the steering wheel into his arms, took her to the SUV and laid her on the passenger seat.

Conor reached across her to crank up the heat, closed that door, ran back to the sedan to turn it off, lock it and pocket the keys before he rushed back behind the wheel of his own vehicle and put it into gear again.

It was a little less than a mile to the cabin. But already the dirt drive was covered in snow and drifts. The only thing Conor could do was go slow enough to feel that his tires were in the wheel ruts, letting them guide him. And hoping like hell that he'd opted for the right road and was headed toward shelter.

Just as he was beginning to doubt it, he caught sight of the small log cabin in the clearing of trees.

Breathing a sigh of relief, he drove the SUV up to the cabin's front porch and stopped. Leaving the engine—and the heat—running for his passenger, he made his way onto the porch and found the key in Rickie's hiding spot. He unlocked the door and entered with a mental thank-you to whoever had used the cabin last and left wood and tinder in the fireplace, ready to be lit.

If only he could find matches.

Matches. Matches. Matches…

After a moment of searching, he finally found a

box of stick matches near a bucket of wood to the side of the hearth.

With a fire going, he returned to the SUV and carefully removed his passenger.

Inside with her, he laid her on the floor in front of the fire, letting the hard wooden surface act as the backboard he would have used had he had one.

She was breathing without any problems—that was good.

As he covered her with a blanket from the worn sofa nearby, the woman groaned.

"Good girl," he praised. "Come on, come to…"

But when she didn't stir again, he ran outside to turn off the SUV and then returned to survey the territory.

With the exception of shelter, the cabin didn't likely offer much in terms of medical tools or supplies. Rickie had assured him that there was plenty of bottled water so Conor went in search of that, a cloth of some sort to clean the wound as best he could and a first-aid kit.

Returning to his patient—who was moaning again— he saw that bleeding from her head wound was increasing as she warmed up.

Working fast, he dampened the cloth with the bottled water and cleaned the wound.

"Can you wake up for me?" he urged. "Come on, open your eyes…"

More moaning but her eyes remained closed.

The wound was a clean cut free of debris. It could have used a couple of stitches but he had to settle for three butterfly bandages covered with a compression wrap.

Then he wet the cloth again to clean her face and

get the hair away from it. The more he saw of her, the more he was struck by that sense of familiarity.

Her hair was thick and lush and the color of a new penny—he hadn't registered that before but now he did.

Red hair.

Maicy had had hair like that…

Just as that thought struck him, the woman opened her emerald green eyes.

Conor reared back and froze.

It couldn't be.

Could it?

No, it couldn't be. It just wasn't possible for the woman coming to on the floor in front of him to be the girl he'd left behind.

And yet the more closely he looked at her, the more he knew it was…

Everything was hazy. Maicy's mind, her senses, were slowly fading in from darkness. She could hear a voice but she couldn't quite make out words. And she felt too heavy to move.

Her head hurt. And she was lying on something hard.

Why would that be?

She remembered that she'd been in her car…

And it had been cold. So cold.

And then, too, there was that voice. A man.

She faded in a little more and blinked open her eyes. Her vision was blurry, and the light seemed dim. There *was* a man there…

"Good girl! Come on, wake up."

This time she heard the words.

But she still couldn't quite focus her eyes. And she

was so disoriented that for a minute the sound of the man's voice actually made her think of Conor Madison. As if *that* made any sense...

"Can you tell me your name?" the man asked.

Definitely not Conor Madison, then—he would know her.

"Maicy," she managed.

"How about your last name, Maicy?"

"Clark," she muttered.

She heard him say, "Holy..." under his breath before shifting back into a calm, professional tone to ask, "Can you tell me what year it is?"

"A new year. January..." The date rolled off her tongue.

But maybe that wasn't the right date. Maybe she only said it out of habit. She'd given that particular date a million times in the last few months while planning the wedding.

The wedding...

"How old are you?" the man asked.

These questions were dumb. "Old enough," she said peevishly.

She pinched her eyes closed against the pain in her head and reached up to feel the source. She discovered that her hair was damp and that there were bandages of some sort on her forehead, just below her hairline.

"Good, you can move your right arm. How about this side?" the man asked, taking her other hand. "Can you squeeze my hand?"

She did that. He had a big hand.

"Strength is good," he decreed. "How about your feet? Can you flex those for me?"

She did as he asked and felt that her feet were bare.

Bare feet? She didn't leave home in her bare feet. Her wedding shoes...

"Where are my shoes—I love those shoes!"

He didn't answer her question. Instead he asked, "Can you tell me what happened to you?"

She opened her eyes again. Her vision was a bit clearer this time, and the fuzzy image of the man on his knees beside her looked even more like her old boyfriend.

This really was bizarre.

"There was a deer. I swerved to miss hitting him," she said, remembering. She also recalled that it was her wedding she'd come from.

And Gary...

"What's around my neck?" she asked when she also became aware that there was something there.

"My coat," the man answered. "Are you experiencing pain anywhere?"

"My head."

"Anywhere else?"

"No."

"Any pain in your neck? Your shoulders? Your back or arms?"

"No."

"I'm going to pinch you a little bit—tell me if you can feel it."

He did, pinching different spots on her arms and legs. She could feel it so she told him so.

Then he said, "Can you raise your legs? One at a time?"

She did that, feeling satin around them. The wedding dress. From the wedding that hadn't been. Because she'd run away from it...

"Okay, very carefully, I want you to try to move your head—can you do that?"

She could do that, too.

"Any pain with that? Any tingling in your shoulders, arms or legs?"

"No."

"Good. I'm going to unwrap your neck but I'm going to do it slowly, if you feel *anything* out of the ordinary, you tell me right away, okay?"

He came closer to unwrap his coat and her vision cleared more so she could take a better look at him.

He had dark hair the color of a double espresso—short on the sides, longer on top—and a handsome face even at that odd angle.

In spite of it she could still tell that his nose was slightly long and flat across the bridge but worked well with the sharp lines of a great bone structure—high cheekbones and a strong jawline and chin.

All refined and tougher versions of what she remembered of the young Conor...

Why did he keep coming to mind?

"Nothing? No pain—shooting or otherwise?" the man asked.

"No," she said softly as she went on assessing his face and finding more and more that reminded her of the boy she'd loved.

And learned to wish she hadn't...

Those full lips.

Those thick eyebrows, the same dark brown as his hair.

Even his ears...

Conor had had really nice ears...

Then her neck was free and he raised his eyes to her face.

And that was when she knew for sure.

No one she'd ever met except the Madison siblings had eyes like that. Bluer than blue, with silver streaks in them.

"Oh my God!" she said in alarm.

"What? Pain? Numbness?" he asked with more urgency.

"You're Conor Madison," she accused.

He relaxed and nodded. "Hi, Maicy," he said calmly.

"I get it—I've died and gone to hell," she muttered.

As much as she'd wanted to escape her own wedding today, she wanted to get away from Conor even more. So she started to sit up.

"Whoa! Whoa! Whoa!" He held her down by the shoulders. "I don't want you moving at all yet, let alone like that!"

"And we know that what you want is all that counts."

He didn't address that. He only said, "It's important that I make sure you don't aggravate any injuries. So please, just let me check you out?"

"I guess that means you *did* become a doctor?" she said, curious but trying to hide it.

"I did. So let me do my job," he reiterated.

Begrudgingly, she conceded to that, doing some checking out of her own as he continued his examination.

Conor Madison. How, on this day of all days, could she open her eyes and find herself with him?

Maybe she was hallucinating. That would be so much better...

But if she was hallucinating, wouldn't she see him as

the boy he'd been when they were last together rather than this solid, muscular, all-grown-up version of him?

The man who was fully developed—broad of chest and shoulders, with biceps that filled and tested the sleeves of the gray sweatshirt he had on.

He'd aged from youthful good looks into a striking handsomeness.

That aggravated Maicy all the more...

"Shouldn't you be wearing a uniform?" she asked with some impudence.

"I'm on leave," he answered curtly as he took her pulse.

His voice was the same. It had been deep then and it was deep now. But now it held more confidence, more certainty, more authority, as he told her what to do.

"I'm fine," she insisted when his examination seemed finished.

"You aren't *completely* fine," he said. "You were in a car accident, you have a gash in your head and were unconscious for some amount of time. If I had you in a hospital I'd send you for X-rays and a CT scan. But since we aren't in a hospital—"

"Where *are* we?" she said.

"The Dale family's hunting cabin."

"Rickie Dale?" She hadn't thought of him in years.

"Right—glad to see that you seem to be firing on all burners. That's a good sign when there's the potential for a brain injury."

"And how is it that I'm here with you?" she asked derisively, thinking that she'd answered enough of his questions and followed enough of his instructions to have earned some reciprocity.

"I was headed for Northbridge when the storm hit,

and I knew I wouldn't make it. I called Rickie and asked if I could use the place now, to wait out this weather. I came across your car on my way here."

"My car…" Maicy said. "Did I wreck it?"

"You were nose-first in a ditch."

Maicy closed her eyes again, overwhelmed for a moment by all this day had brought with it.

"Hey! You aren't passing out on me again, are you?" Conor said in a louder voice.

She opened her eyes. "No," she said, hating that there was gloom in her own tone for him to hear. "It's just been a bad day," she added, hoping he'd leave it at that.

No such luck.

"Yeah, I'd say so… Were you on your way *to* your wedding or coming from it?"

"Neither." She just wasn't sure how to qualify it. "I got to the church but left before the wedding happened."

"Without a coat?"

"I took my coat—it's in the back seat with my suitcase. I just didn't put it on. I was in a hurry."

He didn't push it. Instead he said, "Do you feel like you can sit up?"

"Sure," she answered, not revealing that she felt unsteady and drained because she didn't want him to know there was any weakness in her at all. Not now or ever again.

"I want you to take it slow," he told her. "Let me help you, and tell me immediately if you feel any hint of pain or tingling or numbness."

"Yeah, yeah, yeah," she clipped out.

He helped her sit up, and she made it there without

saying anything, containing the groan that almost escaped when her head throbbed with the movement. Her expression must have shown her pain, though, because he said, "There's some pain reliever in the first-aid kit but I don't want to give you that until I know that the bleeding is under control. Can you stand to wait?"

"Yes." And even if she hadn't been able to, she wouldn't have told him. "Now can I get off this floor?"

"Give it a minute. Let's see what sitting here does first."

Maicy sighed, feeling impatient. Methodical and cautious. That was Conor Madison. To a fault.

And she *had* faulted him for it. With good reason.

Glancing down, Maicy noticed her dress.

"Oh, I'm a mess..." she lamented. And it had been such a beautiful dress—white satin, scooped neck with cowl-like draping to the hem that ended at her ankles in front and gracefully expanded into a short train in back. Now it was wrinkled, soiled and stained with blood.

"Actually, you look pretty damn good..." Conor said. She might have been flattered if she'd been willing to accept a compliment from the likes of him.

But as it was she ignored the remark and announced once more, "I feel fine. Now can I get up?"

"How's the dizziness?"

"Good. Gone," she lied. "I'm sure I can drive. All I have to do is get to my car and back it out of the ditch and—"

He looked at her as if she was crazy. "In the first place," he said, "you're *not* fine—you're doing well, but you are not *unscathed*. You're nowhere near ready to go outside into the snow without shoes or a coat, much less to hike a mile to your car—because that's where it is, at the end of the drive up to this cabin. It's not drivable even if you could get to it—it's going to need a tow truck. Then there's the fact that if you were in an emergency room where you belong, they'd admit you to keep an eye on you overnight, and there is no way in hell I'd let you drive even if this was a balmy summer day. So no matter how you want to cut it, you, Maicy Clark, are stuck here. With me."

Oh…it was worse than she thought. Not only had she encountered the one person she'd hoped never to see again in her life, she was stranded with him?

"You look sick—what's going on?" he said.

"What's going on is that I don't want to be here." *With you!* she added in her head.

But what she said was, "I don't see mine, but surely you have a cell phone—call for help! Maybe somebody could come and get me—an ambulance, or the fire department." She refused to believe that things were as impossible as he claimed.

"If I couldn't get *in* to town, no one can get out," he reasoned.

"I don't want to be here with you!" she blurted, unable to stop herself this time.

"I get that," he said. "But right now we have to do what we have to do. And arguing about it will only waste time we don't have to spare. This place is *not* a four-star hotel and we're going to have to work to stay warm and fed. So if you think you're doing okay enough for me to get you onto the couch, there are some things I need to do to get this place up and running—as much as it runs—in order to get us through tonight."

Tonight? They'd be spending the whole night together in this cabin?

Could this day possibly get any worse?

First her wedding had become a disaster.

And now here she was, isolated and alone with the guy who had broken her heart and abandoned her in her most desperate time of need.

Oh yeah, it definitely would have been better if she were just hallucinating.

Maicy took a deep breath, rallied the strength she'd had to find in herself years before and said, "I can get to the couch myself."

He ignored that.

Which was good because once he'd helped her to her feet her knees buckled and she nearly collapsed.

He caught her in strong, powerful arms that—if she'd had even an iota of strength herself—she would have slapped away.

As it was she had no choice but to let him help her to the sofa.

Once she was there, she shrugged out of his grip and swore to herself that if she couldn't get back up again without his help, she would stay rooted to that spot.

Because the last thing she would ever do again was lean on Conor Madison.

Chapter Two

"Dammit!" Conor shouted into the wind.

After trying several different locations outside, he'd found a spot where he had cell phone reception... temporarily. It lasted long enough to reach his brother's doctor and learn that Declan's fever was rising. Then he'd lost service again. And no matter where he went now, the phone showed no signal.

Meanwhile, the storm was worsening. Now that it was dark the temperature had plummeted, and the wind was howling and making the snow a whirling dervish that was even more impossible to see through.

So Conor turned his attention to the other reason he'd bundled up to come outside—firewood.

He circled to the back of the cabin where the woodpile was, staying close to the log structure so as not to risk losing his bearings. But he was far less worried for himself than he was for his brother.

He'd heard the stories about the shoddy, outdated conditions of some stateside veterans' hospitals, constantly understaffed and undersupplied. And since he'd been back with Declan, he'd seen it for himself. Doctors and nurses were stretched thinner than Conor knew they should be, and he had to put pressure on them to make sure his brother had what he needed.

Was Declan's care suffering now that he wasn't there to keep an eye on things?

Why the hell had he thought it was a good idea to leave Declan's side in the first place?

But Declan had been doing so well and they'd both known that one of them had to get to Kinsey to talk some sense into her before she shook up their lives with her quest to build a relationship with the family they hadn't known they had.

For cripes sake, Kinsey, why couldn't you just leave well enough alone? Who cares if Mitchum Camden was our biological father? We were just his dirty secret, hidden away from his high-society wife and family while he carried on with Mom behind their backs all those years.

They'd barely even seen the man while he was still alive. And after he died—in a plane crash with various other members of his family—their mom had eventually moved on. She'd married their stepdad, the man who truly raised them. And she'd never told any of her children about their father…until her deathbed confession to Kinsey.

Now Kinsey was determined to build a relationship with Mitchum Camden's other children. And neither Conor, Declan nor Declan's twin, Liam, were on board with that. She was determined to build a relationship the Camdens didn't seem to want, either.

With Declan laid up and Liam on special assignment overseas with his own marine unit, the job of dissuading their sister had fallen to Conor. But since the weather was keeping him from meeting Kinsey, this trip was a complete waste.

Well, maybe not a complete waste since it did put him here to save Maicy.

But still, thinking about what he *should* be doing for his brother made frustration hit him all over again. Frustration that piled on top of the uneasiness that had been dogging him for a while.

Initially in his career he'd liked the excitement, the speed, the exhilaration of emergency and trauma medicine, of being the first person to treat injured military men and women, to safeguard their lives just as they safeguarded the world with their service. But the longer it went on, the more it had begun to eat at him that it wasn't up to him to give extended care, to see his patients through and make sure their ongoing treatment was successful. Declan was the first patient he'd been able to stay with—and now he was letting his brother down.

Conor reached the woodpile and, with a vengeance born out of those frustrations, threw back the tarp covering it.

There's nothing you can do about it! he told himself firmly. Nothing he could do about Declan or about any of the hundreds of military men and women whose treatment it was his job only to begin.

Nothing he could do other than continuing to look

for a phone signal at any rate, so he could stay on top of Declan's care from here, no matter what it took.

It didn't ease his anxiousness a lot, but at least having a plan, setting a course of any kind, helped a little.

And in the meantime he had to deal with the situation he was currently in.

Which was also one hell of a situation.

The cabin was stocked for the winter with plenty of already-cut wood, bottled water and nonperishable food. Nothing luxurious, but enough to keep them safe.

Maicy was more of a problem.

So far it appeared that she didn't have a serious brain injury, that she had a minor concussion that a little rest would cure. But if she took a turn for the worse like Declan and the storm, they were going to have bigger problems.

Bigger even than the fact that it *was* Maicy Clark he was stranded with—the one person in the world who had every reason to hate his guts. And apparently did.

Sometimes it just sucked to do what he thought was right, what he thought was best for everyone involved.

And when it came to Maicy it had left him with guilt he could never dislodge.

Not even now, when it didn't seem as if she had done too badly for herself.

After all, the car she'd crashed into the ditch had been a high-end sedan, and looking at her...

Despite her injury, she *looked* great—certainly not world-weary or worn or as if life had gotten the better of her.

She'd always had that amazing head of hair—thick and wavy and shiny. It used to feel like heavy silk whenever he'd gotten his hands into it, and it was no less lush now.

And that face? Time had *not* taken a toll on that, either. Instead it had only improved on perfection, removing the girlish immaturity and leaving her an incredibly beautiful woman.

Her skin was like porcelain and her features were delicate and refined, with elegant, high cheekbones, a thin, graceful nose, and soft ruby lips that he'd never been able to get his fill of.

And if that wasn't enough—along with the lush way her compact little body had blossomed—there were those eyes.

Sparkling, vibrant, emerald green.

One look from those eyes in days gone by and he would have moved mountains for her...

Though he had managed to stand his ground that one time. And from what she said, it was clear she had not forgiven or forgotten. Never mind that the choice he'd made all those years ago had been every bit as much about what he'd thought was best for her as what he'd known he had to do himself. He'd still hurt her.

And now he had to contend with the fallout.

All these years later.

Alone in a small space with her and all of her anger.

The young Maicy had been a sweetheart. Uncomplicated and good-natured, agreeable and soft-hearted. But now? Somewhere along the way some spunk and feistiness had been added. And a touch of temper to go with that red hair. Cut and bloodied and reeling and barely conscious again, she'd still shot barbs at him and had seemed very prepared to make his life miserable until they could get out of here.

But like having unreliable cell phone service, when it came to Maicy he was just going to have to do what he could and cope, he told himself as he picked up the canvas sling that he'd filled with as much wood as it would hold.

And maybe he needed to use this strange opportunity to see if he could finally explain why he had denied her request—an explanation she hadn't listened to eighteen years ago.

It might not make any difference, he thought as he inched along the rear of the cabin to get to the back door again, but he'd like to try.

Because along with the other things that were eating at him lately there had also come some wondering, some questioning, about his own course, his own choices. And if he'd made the right ones.

First and foremost, about Maicy.

Maicy had dozed off, and when she woke up daylight was gone, darkness had fallen, and the only sounds were of the raging storm outside and the fire crackling inside.

"Conor?" she called out. There was no answer.

She sat up on the worn plaid sofa where she'd fallen asleep, keeping the blanket around her and wondering if Conor had deserted her. After all, it wouldn't be the first time.

The couch was under the cabin's front window. Peering through it, beyond the snow blowing like a white sheet in the wind, she thought she could see flashes of his silver SUV. So he had to be around somewhere.

Her head hurt and she reached up to feel the bandaging. The blood had begun to dry. She assumed that meant the gash must have stopped bleeding. But her whole body was more stiff and sore than it had been before. And she felt weak. Drained.

Hard to tell whether that was from her physical condition or her mental state, she thought.

She slumped back against the soft cushions, studying her surroundings in the dim firelight.

She'd never been to this cabin before. Rickie had brought friends out for camping or hunting, but never for parties—and now she could see why. Built by Rickie's great-great-grandfather, the place provided shelter but it was hardly a showpiece.

The living room she was in featured rough-hewn log walls and a wood-planked floor, the old couch she was on and a scarred coffee table. Off to one side, the kitchen section was made up of a small utility table acting as an island counter and a few cupboards. There was also an old black-and-silver wood-burning stove in the corner, but that was it—no refrigerator, no other appliances at all.

A doorway off the kitchen led somewhere she couldn't see into, and another to Maicy's left appeared to be a bedroom with a four-poster bed that looked old enough to have arrived by covered wagon.

If there was a bathroom, she couldn't see it from the sofa and she worried that the only facilities might be an outhouse.

All in all, it was nothing like the cozy, quaint bridal suite at the Northbridge Bed-and-Breakfast, where she'd planned to spend tonight.

Instead she was here. A runaway bride.

What a mess this had all become…

Rather than being at her wedding reception tonight,

dancing and celebrating as Mrs. Gary Stern, she and Gary were over. And as if that wasn't bad enough, she was stranded in a log cabin with yet another, earlier example of her lousy taste in men.

"I keep thinking I'm making better choices than you did, Mom, but maybe I inherited some kind of faulty man-reader from you," she muttered.

There was no question that her mother had chosen poorly in Maicy's father. At the first sign of any problem—big or small—John Clark had taken off. Disappeared, sometimes for a year or two at a time.

Her mother had excused him, saying their shotgun marriage after her mother had discovered she was pregnant with Maicy had not been easy for him. Maicy hadn't had much sympathy.

To her, her father had been a drop-in houseguest whom her mother waited—and waited and waited—for. A man who never stayed long before he was gone again.

And every time he left, her mother had sunk into dark depressions that lasted for months.

Once, Maicy had asked why her mother didn't divorce him and find someone who would be there for her. For them both.

Her mother's only answer had been that she loved the man.

That had seemed silly to twelve-year-old Maicy.

Until she'd fallen in love herself.

With Conor.

Sitting sideways on the sofa, she pulled her knees to her chest and huddled under the blanket, staring into the fire now, wondering where he'd gone.

Conor was as unreliable as her father, she reminded herself. As untrustworthy.

But Gary? She'd thought there was no risk with him.

Steady, conservative, hometown Gary.

Gary, who had been hurt as badly by love as she had.

Gary, who she'd been convinced was predictable and safe...

Oh yeah, she definitely had a faulty man-reader.

She wasn't sure if it made things better or worse that she hadn't been wholeheartedly in love with Gary, the way she'd been with Conor. When she'd caught him today, she'd still been angry. Hurt. Embarrassed.

But she was also secretly relieved.

And now, sitting alone in the aftermath, she couldn't help wondering why that was—because relieved was still how she felt.

"I really need to talk to you, Rach," she muttered, wishing she had her cell phone to call her friend.

Everything was just such a mess...

Pain shot through her gashed forehead just then, forcing her eyes closed until it passed.

If the bleeding had stopped or at least slowed down, maybe she could finally take something for the pain.

"Conor?" she called, hoping maybe he'd hear her from wherever he was—maybe there was a basement or a cellar or something...

But still there was no answer.

Where *was* he?

It occurred to her suddenly that if he was outside in this storm, maybe something had happened to him.

That sent a strong wave of alarm through her and she got up.

Too fast.

Her head went into such a spin that she fell back onto the sofa.

"Okay, that wasn't great," she said out loud.

She waited, took some deep breaths, tried to relax. The dizziness began to pass.

But the worry that something might have happened to Conor didn't. She had to see if he was okay.

She got up again, this time much more carefully. She was definitely weak. Her knees felt as if they might give out.

But she wasn't going to let that happen. She did what she'd been doing since the day Conor had left her on her own—she willed herself to push through. Pain, weakness, fear, depression, whatever—she stood on her own two feet regardless!

And now that she was on those two feet all she needed to do was go to the other side of the room. That was nothing, she told herself.

She wrapped the blanket around her shoulders like a cape and clutched it in front with one hand. Keeping her other hand against the wall for support, she took careful steps, aiming for the other side of the room and the window over the kitchen sink. Hoping as she did that she wouldn't discover Conor outside, hurt or incapacitated in some way. Because she was in no shape to rescue him.

Along the way she reached the doorway off the kitchen and found that there was another small room with a door leading outside.

The room appeared to be a catchall—a pantry stocked with food and a supply room where she saw snowshoes and a shovel and an ax among other things.

Other things that didn't include Conor.

So she bypassed the room and finished the trip to the kitchen sink.

When she got there she maintained her grip on the blanket with one hand and held on to the edge of the sink with the other.

"Wow," she said as she peered out the window at the storm. She'd seen some bad ones, but this topped the list.

Just then the snow swirled away from the cabin and she caught sight of something moving to the left.

She craned forward, looking hard through the window. There was definitely someone out there. Someone big. It had to be him. Maybe at a woodpile? Getting firewood made sense.

Feeling relieved, she turned and slowly retraced her steps back to the couch as a slight shiver shook her. Even with her blanket cape, the blood-soaked wedding dress was *not* the warmest of attires.

The sofa was a welcome respite when she got there again. Sitting at one end she pulled her knees up to her chest, tightened the blanket around herself so every inch was covered and returned to staring into the fire that was the only source of heat.

Her short venture had used up the little oomph she'd had and she rested her head to the back of the sofa cushion, thinking that it was a good thing Conor *didn't* need her help.

And what kind of a weird practical joke was fate playing on her today, anyway? First Gary's old flame dropped into his lap and now hers?

She closed her eyes at that thought and made a face.

She did *not* like the way things had gone with Conor so far. Most of all, she didn't like that she'd lost control over her emotions. She hadn't even realized she was still that angry with him. What had happened with him was ancient history. She'd come to grips with it long ago, chalking it up to experience. It had taken her some time—well into adulthood, actually—but she'd even come to think that he'd probably made the right decision. How many teenage marriages actually worked out?

So, if it was all water under the bridge—which it was—why hadn't she just been indifferent, detached, completely unemotional toward him?

She should have been. Instead, she'd been anything *but*. The only explanation she had for it was that today had just thrown too much at her. Seeing Conor again had been the straw that broke the camel's back...even if he happened to be the person who had kept her from dying today.

The person she should have been grateful to.

She chafed at that thought.

Grateful to Conor Madison?

This really was a practical joke on fate's part—now she had to be *grateful* to the guy who had dumped her?

Fabulous, she thought facetiously.

But she also wasn't happy to have behaved so poorly toward Conor.

Not that he didn't deserve her scorn and contempt. But showing it put her in a position she didn't want to be in. She didn't want to be the smaller person. The grudge-bearer.

And she didn't want him thinking she cared.

So that lashing-out thing wasn't going to happen from here on, she vowed. Not when it might make him think she hadn't gotten over him. That their childhood romance had been so important to her that she was still hurt or mad or something. Anything.

Because she wasn't.

It wasn't as if she would ever choose to be stuck in a snowstorm, in a small space with him, but since she apparently couldn't alter that, she wasn't going to let it be a big deal. She was just going to make the best of it until this all passed.

Then they would part ways again.

But in the meantime he was not going to get to her. He was basically a stranger to her now. A stranger whose company she would have to endure for a little while whether she liked it or not.

A stranger who had grown into one of the best-looking men she'd ever seen...

That didn't matter, either.

Even if it *was* the truth.

He'd always been handsome, only somehow time and a few years had done wonders for him. It had taken chiseled features and added some hardcore masculinity and a ruggedness that screamed raw sensuality. It had built even more muscle mass onto his body and turned him into a hunk-and-a-half.

But it really didn't matter. Not to her. It didn't have any effect on her. *He* didn't have any effect on her.

So move on, storm, she commanded.

Because as soon as it did, she could get out of this place and put Conor Madison back in the past, where he belonged.

When the back door opened she knew it. The sound of the screeching wind wasn't muffled and a frigid blast of air whipped through the cabin.

Maicy didn't budge. She just went from looking at the fire to watching for Conor to appear through that door.

Finally, he came into view. Snow and droplets of water dotted dark hair that was in unfairly attractive disarray. The collar of his navy blue peacoat was turned up to frame his sexy jawline, and the coat accentuated shoulders a mile wide now.

But none of it was going to have an impact on her, she told herself.

"You're awake," he said when his eyes met hers.

"I am," she confirmed, forcing her tone to be completely dispassionate and neutral. "What time is it?"

"Almost ten. How do you feel?"

"I'm okay," she insisted, unwilling to confide more in him.

"I need to know, Maicy," he reprimanded, so she told him the details, still assuring him she was fine, but adding that she wouldn't mind a little pain reliever for her headache.

"And I don't suppose you brought my suitcase from my car when you got me out, did you?" she asked, huddling in the blanket.

"I didn't," he said, leaving his coat in place as he brought firewood around the utility table. "I was only paying attention to you—I didn't even notice anything else in the car. I have my duffel, though. You can wear something of mine when you're up to changing—something warm."

"I'd appreciate that," she said even though she wasn't thrilled with the prospect of wearing his clothes. And while she was at it, she said, "And I also appreciate what you did getting me here. You saved me. Thank you for that."

"Any time—" he said before cutting himself off as if he only just remembered that their past made that promise into a lie.

He turned from her to arrange the firewood, and Maicy's gaze went to his thighs stretching the denim of his jeans to capacity—thick and solid.

"If you're up to it," he said as he loaded the bucket, "there are some logistics we should discuss."

"Okay," Maicy agreed.

"We're pretty socked in by this storm," he began. "Cell service is spotty—at best. I get service one minute, lose it the next. And until this storm quits, I don't know when we'll be able to get out of here."

"Tomorrow—"

"I think that may be optimistic and we have to plan for a little longer than that."

"How long?" she asked, trying to keep her distaste for that idea out of her tone.

"I don't know. I just know that we have to conserve supplies, just in case. It's impossible to tell at this point how long we'll be here, but better safe than sorry."

Maicy clenched her teeth to keep from making a snide comment about that being his guiding rule.

"Here's how it is up here," he continued. "We're off the grid. That means no electricity, limited water. The water in the storage tank downstairs is the only non-drinking water, and the only power we have comes from a solar-powered generator. Both of those are at about half capacity. I can get us by for a while with what we have, but only if we're careful. The water in the tank isn't for eating or drinking but there's plenty of bottled water for that. We have a pretty good stock of dried and canned food. The woodpile is high—

that's good. But, for instance, something like taking a shower—"

"No showers?" Maicy said in horror, thinking of how sticky she felt with the blood in her hair and down her neck.

"Yes, showers, but here's how they happen—there's a propane tank hooked to the water heater in the basement. I can turn on the gas and heat the water but every time I do that, we're using up propane and water. So to shower it'll take half an hour to heat the water. Then, in the shower, there's a chain to pull to turn the pump on and off. You pull the chain, get wet, stop the water. Lather up. Pull the chain to rinse off. All as quick as possible so you use as little water as you can."

"Okay…" she said, already missing the long, steamy showers she ordinarily took. But trying to look on the bright side, she said, "So this must mean that there *is* a bathroom?"

"There's a room," he hedged. "Off the bedroom. That's where the shower is, along with a composting toilet."

"I don't know what that is."

"It's a john that'll take some explanation, too. But it *looks* like a regular one, if that helps," he joked, giving her that familiar one-sided smile that had made her feel better about most anything when she'd liked him.

It still worked, damn him.

"I also stocked the bathroom with candles and some kerosene lanterns, so you'll have light in there, anyway," he said.

He was so confident, so sure of himself. No wonder she'd believed in him when she'd been at her most distressed…

"I've been in worse," he concluded. "We'll be fine, we just need to conserve what resources we have." He'd finished with the firewood and he stood up, unbuttoning his coat and taking it off. "Let me get a lantern and check your head," he said next. "Any nausea or are you getting hungry?"

Food was the last thing on her mind. But she said, "I'm not nauseous."

"Good. For tonight I just want to get some food and water in you, and get you to bed."

There wasn't any insinuation in that but still it set off a tiny titillation in her that she tried to tell herself was just the chill.

"Where are you sleeping?" she heard herself ask.

He laughed.

No, no, no, not his laugh. She'd always had a weakness for his laugh, too…

"I'll take the couch," he assured her. "But we're playing hospital tonight so I'll be in every couple of hours to check on you."

And crawl into bed with her and hold her and keep her warm with those massively muscled arms wrapped around her?

Ohhh, that was some weird flashback to the teenage Maicy's fantasies…

A blow to the head… I've suffered a severe blow to the head. It must have knocked something loose…

Something she would make sure was tightened up again.

"We'll deal with everything else tomorrow," she heard him say into the chaos of her thoughts.

"So I can't shower tonight?" she said when that sank in.

"Nope. I'll heat enough on the stove for you to clean

up a little better, but I want you down until tomorrow. We'll see then if you can shower," he decreed, before heading to get the lantern.

And as much as she didn't want to, Maicy couldn't help checking out his walk-away.

That had gotten better, too.

But it's what's inside that counts, she lectured herself.

And she didn't mean what was inside those jeans.

It was what was inside the man that counted.

The man whom she had—once upon a time—asked to marry her.

Only to have him turn her down.

Chapter Three

Maicy would have slept much better on Sunday night had Conor not come in every two hours to check on her—the way he'd warned her he would.

The four-poster bed was the most comfortable thing she'd ever slept on. Conor had given her a brand new T-shirt and sweatpants straight out of the packages to use as pajamas, the sheets were clean, and with two downy quilts covering her and the slowly burning fire in the shared fireplace—that Conor also kept watch over all night—it would have been heavenly if not for her headache, and the interruptions.

She awoke Monday morning to the sound of wood being split outside. Using the blanket that had covered her on the sofa the night before as a robe, she tested her strength and balance rather than bounding out of the bed.

She was still weak and sore in spots, but much better than the night before. So she left the bedroom and went into the kitchen.

Looking out the window over the sink she could see that the wind had calmed slightly, but snow was still falling heavily on top of what looked to be more than two feet already on the ground.

Conor had shoveled a path to the woodpile and was there, splitting logs with the swing of an ax.

That was a sight to wake up to!

One she was leery of standing there to watch.

She was not going to be sucked into admiring the fine specimen of a man he'd become. There was nothing personal between them at all anymore, and that was the way it would stay. Their former connection had died an ugly death. And even before it had, it clearly hadn't been as meaningful to him as it was to her. So what he was doing for her now was merely being a good Samaritan, there wasn't anything else to it.

She just had to stop cataloging—and yeah, okay, admiring—his physical improvements, and make certain that she didn't read anything into his behavior. He was a doctor—taking care of injured women who fell in his path was just part of his job. It didn't mean anything. She didn't *want* it to mean anything. She was indifferent to him now. So she didn't let herself stay at the sink and watch him splitting logs. Instead, she moved across the room to the front window to survey that side of the cabin.

He'd shoveled off the front porch and cleared the snow from his SUV but she wasn't sure why he'd bothered. There was no driving on the road with all that snow.

"Come on, snow, just stop," she beseeched the weather to no avail, plopping down onto the couch dejectedly.

Conor came in not long after and made powdered eggs that weren't too unpalatable, and then removed the dressing from her head.

As he did she said, "So you *did* become a doctor, but what about career military?"

"Yes, that too—so far," he answered as if there was some question to that. But she didn't explore it. Something seemed to be on his mind today, troubling him. He was checking for cell service obsessively and with every failed attempt the frown lines between his eyebrows dug in a little deeper.

But the days of feeling free to just ask him anything, the days of confiding in each other, were long gone.

Once he'd checked her wound and judged that it was healing properly, he cleaned around it, redressed it and sealed it in a makeshift wrapping that allowed her to take a shower and very carefully wash her hair.

It wasn't the best shower or shampoo she'd ever had but it still made her feel worlds better.

Then she put on another pair of Conor's gray sweatpants and a matching gray sweatshirt that were many sizes too big for her but were warm and soft inside.

The trouble was—despite the fact that they were clean—the sweats smelled like Conor.

Not that it was a bad scent. The opposite of that, actually. They carried a scent she remembered vividly, a scent that was somehow clean and soapy yet still all him. A scent she hadn't been able to get enough of when she had feelings for him. A scent that brought back memories that she had to fight like mad to escape.

But fight them she did. And mostly failed.

After a lunch of potato soup made from dried potatoes—and making sure that Maicy was well enough to be left alone for a while—Conor decided to snowshoe down the road that led to the cabin in hopes of finding a cell signal.

He left her with orders to rest but because Maicy felt well enough to look around a bit, she spent the afternoon getting the lay of the land, for her own peace of mind.

It wasn't as if she thought Conor wouldn't come back this time. It was just that her past had taught her to always make sure she could take care of herself in any eventuality.

So she explored the supplies in the mudroom, counting bottles of water and calculating how long they would last, and learning what types and quantities of foodstuff were available.

She located flashlights, lanterns and kerosene, an abundance of candles, boxes of matches, more snowshoes, heavy gloves she hoped she never had to put her hands into because they were pretty gross-looking, and a second ax.

She even opened the back door and stuck her head out so she could get an idea of how to reach the woodpile from there.

Then she found the stairs that went from the mudroom to the basement and she made her way down.

She checked everything out, read the instructions attached to the generator so she could feel as if she had a working knowledge of its operation. She located the two extra propane tanks and studied how the one that was currently attached to the water heater could be replaced if necessary. She also discovered where Conor had come up with the additional blankets and pillows that he'd used to sleep on the couch.

Then she returned upstairs and opened every cupboard door to see what was inside, figured out how to work the wood-burning stove, and decided she was going to make the evening meal—canned chili and cornbread from a mix.

The only thing she didn't go through was Conor's duffel bag. But as daylight was waning and he still hadn't come back, she began to plan what she would do if he didn't return. How she could use a pair of the snowshoes that were in the mudroom and layer on more of the clothes he must have in his duffel, if she needed to go in search of him.

But then she heard stomping on the porch just before the front door opened and in came Conor.

He was so covered in snow that he barely looked human, bringing with him her suitcase, purse and the pink cake box she'd snatched from her wedding when she'd run out of the church basement.

"You went to my car?" she exclaimed, thrilled to have access to her own things—especially to clothes that didn't smell like him.

"I was almost there before I got cell reception, figured I might as well go the rest of the way to get your stuff." He set everything down, took off his gloves and coat and opened the front door again to shake the snow from them before laying them near the fire to dry.

"You kept the fire going—that's good. I didn't think I'd be out this long. And what are you doing over there? You're supposed to be resting," he said, surveying things.

"I'm fine," she insisted. "I'm cooking. And you brought dessert."

"I did?"

"That pink box. It's the top tier to the wedding cake. My friend Rachel Walsh made it. We met in college."

"I wondered what that was. I just figured I'd bring everything I found. I have to make a confession and ask a favor, though," he added.

"What?"

"I, uh… I got into your purse to find your cell phone."

Maicy did not like the idea that he'd gone through her purse. But there was something grim in his attitude as he removed his boots and put those by the fire, too, so she curbed her own reaction to that and gave him an excuse. "Were you thinking that mine might work better up here than yours?"

"I already tried that on the way back. It doesn't. But the favor I need is for your phone to be a backup so when my battery is drained, I can use yours while I recharge in the car—which we shouldn't do often because we don't want the car battery and the gas depleted, either."

"Bottom line," Maicy said, "is that even if I can get service on mine at some point, you don't want me to use it."

He bent over so his head was toward the fire and ran his hands through his hair to rub the water out of it with a punishing force.

Maicy couldn't help the glance at his rear end—until she realized that was what she was doing. Then she put a stop to it by putting the cornbread in the oven.

When she turned back to the utility table Conor was standing with his back to the fire, apparently to get warm.

"I'm sort of sitting on a powder keg," he told her.

"And the phones—for what little good they're doing—are my only hope."

A single explanation occurred to Maicy and it hit her hard enough to make her blurt out, "You have a pregnant wife somewhere who could deliver any minute."

And why had there been a note of horror in her voice?

Or, for that matter, horror at the thought. *She'd* been about to get married. She *would* be married right now had things gone differently. Why was it unthinkable that he might be?

But it didn't matter. She still hated the idea.

"No. I'm not married and nobody is pregnant," he said as if he didn't know why she would even suggest such a thing.

"Do you *have* kids?" Another burst she couldn't stop.

"No," he repeated, adding a challenging, "Do you?"

"No."

"This is about Declan," he said then, getting back to the issue.

"Your brother," Maicy said, trying to follow what he was saying while gathering her scattered thoughts.

"Declan was hurt in Afghanistan a few months back. In an IED explosion," Conor explained.

"That's a bomb, right? An IED?"

"Right. It stands for improvised explosive device."

"And he lived?"

"He did, thank God. But he's been critical for a long time—"

"I'm so sorry. Is he going to be all right?"

"I thought so. I took leave time to follow him from hospital to hospital to make sure everything was done right—he was so messed up that I worried something minor might be overlooked while his major injuries were being dealt with."

Some things about Conor clearly hadn't changed—like his need to control any potential problems.

"I wasn't going to let that happen," he added.

She'd heard that from him before.

"I can't treat family," he was saying, "but I could damn sure be with him through it all and get *everything* that needed to be done, done."

The *right* way—it wasn't what he said but for Maicy it was an echo from the past.

The right way according to Conor.

He definitely hadn't changed, which left Maicy with no doubt that he'd been vigilant on his brother's behalf.

"We've been stateside for two weeks and he was doing well enough that he wanted me to make this trip to meet Kinsey in Northbridge. Yesterday I checked with him the minute the plane landed. He sounded a little off to me, but he said he was okay. On the way up here—before I lost service—I called again and discovered that he'd developed a fever."

"Not good," Maicy said, interpreting his dire tone.

"*Really* not good," he confirmed. "A fever that comes on that fast is a red flag on its own. But then I couldn't get through again until today and when I did, the news was what I was afraid of—he has sepsis."

"I don't know what that is."

"You've heard of blood poisoning?"

"Sure."

"Well, that's sepsis. An infection has gotten into his blood stream, and depending on how his body fights it and how it's treated, it could kill him. He hasn't gone into septic shock but he's back in intensive care, and he could go into shock in the blink of an eye and—"

"You're trying to keep tabs on what's going on with him."

He nodded. "I have to stay on top of it. VA hospitals here are overcrowded—the staff doesn't have enough time for sufficient individual care. I can't let Declan go down because something gets missed or mishandled. Plus he's allergic to a lot of the antibiotics it would be best to use and I need to make sure he gets the combination he can tolerate that's still strong enough to give him a chance."

"I'm so sorry," Maicy repeated because she didn't know what else to say.

"I should have gone with my gut and stayed with him," Conor said, more to himself than to her. "But there's been stuff with Kinsey and…" He sighed disgustedly. "And then I was up here, stuck in this damn storm."

Ooo. Maicy had never heard him curse the way he did following that statement. He was really upset.

Collecting himself, he shook his head, drawing back those broad shoulders and stiffening up as if it helped contain some of his stress. "I also got through to Rickie while I had service to see if he could get up here, if he could get me to somewhere I could fly out of."

"Could he?" Maicy asked hopefully.

"Not any chance in hell," he said with disgust. "The Billings airport is still closed—along with most of Billings—and now so is the highway between here and there. And there's been an avalanche and rock-slide just outside of Northbridge, on the only road in or out. That'll keep everybody stuck there until the storm passes. Then they'll have to bulldoze through the slide before anybody will be able to get to us from that direction. That's why I went the rest of the way for your things—we're looking at being here longer than I thought."

And he was irritated and more shaken up than she'd ever seen him. More like she'd been yesterday when she'd realized what was going on and with whom she was stranded.

Maybe it was her turn to have the cooler head that prevailed, Maicy thought, because Conor looked like he could put a fist through a wall at any moment. And it didn't seem like he'd be deterred by the fact that these weren't just walls, they were tree trunks.

"I'm not a medical person," she said calmly. "I don't know anything about that kind of thing, so help me understand... Do you feel like Declan's doctors are incompetent?"

"No, they're good. They're just overworked. His primary is actually a guy I was with for a while on a tour on an aircraft carrier—Vince Collier. I'd let him treat me."

"So his doctor is competent and conscientious," she said, then, "I know I'm always asked if I'm allergic to anything when I see a doctor, so you must have told everyone about Declan's allergies, right?"

"I made sure it was noted in big letters everywhere, and yeah, I've said it to everyone who's come near him."

"Plus Declan knows his allergies and he hasn't gone into shock, so double-checking his antibiotics is something he can make sure of himself."

"I don't know about that—a fever like he has could leave him confused."

"Okay, but you've been there with Declan, so everyone knows you, too—that you're a navy doctor, that you're keeping an eye on them and everything they do, yes?"

"Yes, but I'm not there to do that now," he said impatiently, as if he didn't see the point of any of what she was asking.

"But the groundwork is laid," she said. "And you've got two brotherhoods working for you—the brotherhood of doctors, and the whole military brotherhood. It seems to me that whether you're there or not, everyone is going to try that much harder not to drop the ball with Declan."

That gave him pause for just a moment before he conceded. "I don't know…maybe… This is just really serious…"

"But you said Declan was doing pretty well before this—it would be worse if this had hit him when he was even weaker, wouldn't it? Now he's in good enough shape for you to feel like you *could* leave him, so he must have a little bit to fight this with."

"Sepsis is dangerous no matter what," he insisted.

"And if you were there with him, what would you be doing?"

"Keeping watch!" he said, again as if she was clueless.

"And you'd see a lot of people doing their jobs—which is what's still happening. Sitting in a chair in his room would make you feel better, but it wouldn't necessarily change anything," she reasoned. "So yes, we'll keep my phone as backup and you'll still keep trying to get through so you can put your two cents' worth in, but maybe you can trust—at least a little— that you've gotten Declan this far and put him in the best position, and whatever he needs will be done now with or without you being there?"

Conor drew his hands through his hair again, pulling so hard on his scalp that he yanked his head back and glared at the ceiling.

From her vantage point Maicy saw his upturned jaw clench and she wondered if she'd pushed too far, if reason wasn't what he'd wanted to hear.

Then he took a deep breath and sighed hard as he dropped his hands and brought his head down again to look at her.

"Yeah, you're right," he admitted. "About all of that. And I did talk to Collier for a few minutes before the phone cut out again. I think—*think*—he's doing what he should. It's just that this is really bad," he said in a tone that was thick with fear and worry. "And I should be there…" His voice dwindled off, letting Maicy see just how much this bothered him.

But before she could think of anything more to say he let out a mirthless chuckle. "I guess this must be what Kinsey feels like with us all in active service— afraid for us and helpless as all hell."

Knowing nothing about what that might be like, Maicy agreed with that observation only with a raise of her eyebrows.

That inspired a shock of pain that reminded her that she was injured. She thought that they were quite a pair stuck here snowbound—her with a head injury and him climbing out of his skin with worry about his brother.

Then Conor drew himself up as if coming to grips

with some of his demons and said, "I'm gonna heat the water and take a quick shower."

"Sure. Good idea," Maicy said.

Conor disappeared downstairs. In the meantime Maicy retrieved her suitcase and purse, feeling as joyful as a kid at Christmas to have them with her again, and took them into the bedroom.

Then she relocated the pink cake box to the kitchen, setting it aside for later.

By the time Conor's shower was finished the cornbread was cooked, the can of chili she'd opened was simmering on the stovetop, she had plates, bowls and bottles of water waiting, and she'd lit some of the candles she'd found in the mudroom to add a little light.

Not in any romantic way, she made sure to tell herself. Just so they could see what they were eating.

What she *wasn't* prepared for was the impact of looking up from her tasks to find the freshly showered and shaved Conor rejoining her in that candlelight.

He was wearing navy blue sweatpants and a matching hoodie with NAVY emblazoned across his expansive chest.

His dark hair was shower-damp. His face was bare of whiskers and even more handsome with all the sculpted lines and planes revealed. And that soapy scent that had tormented her from his clothes wafted out from him and went right to her head.

But only for a minute before she got a hold of herself. She focused on stirring the chili so she didn't have to look at him, thinking that this was a dirty trick on fate's part. If Conor had aged into a troll of a man it would have been bad enough to be in this situation with him. But as it was, his appeal had doubled from what it had been when he was eighteen and this was turning into a constant test of her resistance that she didn't appreciate.

"I'll shut off the propane on the water heater but we should still have enough warm water in the tank to do the dishes," he said as he headed for the basement again.

Maicy didn't respond to that, working to remind herself not to let the way he looked have any effect on her.

She thought she had it under control until he came back. But one glimpse of him rattled her all over again.

It doesn't matter how hot he is, she lectured herself, *think about who he is and what he did.*

Holding fast to memories of old injuries, she ladled out the chili and cut the cornbread, then he took his plate and she took hers to the coffee table to eat, sitting side by side on the sofa, facing the kitchen rather than each other.

After a few bites, Conor said, "Now that you've talked me off the ledge—thanks for that by the way—tell me about this wedding of yours so I can think about something else and stop obsessing over Declan and things I can't do."

Maicy wondered if it had rocked him at all to think of her with someone else—the way it had rocked her earlier when she'd thought he might want cell service to keep up with a pregnant wife. But there were no indications of it.

Before she'd said anything he said, "I know you didn't stay in Northbridge—my mom said you left a year after I did and never came back—but you were getting married there?"

"I got a scholarship to the University of Colorado

in Boulder, I went there for undergrad. Then I got my masters at CU Denver campus and stayed," she explained.

"What did you get your degrees in?"

"Career counseling and development. I own my own career counseling service in Denver."

"So you went to Colorado, live in Denver, but went back to Northbridge to get married?" he said, returning to the original subject.

"A little over a year ago I ran into Gary Stern on the street—"

"That little dorky guy from your graduating class?"

"He evolved out of the dorkiness," she defended even though she didn't feel particularly inclined to support her cheating former fiancé. Granted, she couldn't argue that he wasn't little—only two inches taller than Maicy's own five feet four inches and slight enough that if she'd been wearing Gary's sweatsuit now it would have fit her perfectly.

Then she went on. "He'd just moved away from Northbridge after Candace Jackson turned down *his* proposal."

Okay, there might have been a touch of snideness to that last part, but if Conor had heard it he didn't say anything. He only said, "Candace Jackson… She started out my year, got thrown from a horse and had to be held back into your class because she missed so much school."

"Right. But she's perfectly healthy now…" Maicy said sardonically.

"And she turned down Stern's proposal and he moved to Denver, where you met up with him again and…what? Hit it off?"

Commiserated as two people dumped by high school sweethearts, was more like it.

But that wasn't how Maicy framed it. "At first we were only old friends meeting again after a long time. But then yes, we hit it off, started to date—"

"You and Stern…" he mused, glancing at her in disbelief. "I can't see it."

"We were good together," she said, defensively again. "At least I thought we were. Gary's transition from small town to big city was a little rough, though. He worked as an account manager at a brokerage house but six months in, the company let him go."

"That's not good. How come?"

"They said he just didn't fit in—it was kind of a high-profile firm and it seemed like Gary just didn't have the… I don't know…the panache for their big clients. Anyway, about that time his apartment lease expired and his rent almost doubled from the move-in rate—"

"And being newly unemployed, he couldn't afford it," Conor said for her.

"Right. I was giving him career counseling and trying to help him find work. But Denver's population is booming and there's a lot of competition for every opening—"

"And he wasn't the cream of the crop even with you in his corner."

There *was* a hint of Conor not liking the thought of her with Gary—it was in his tone and that comment.

Maicy found some satisfaction in that.

"Gary was down on his luck," was all she would admit to. "And things between us were going well, so I didn't want to see him move back to Northbridge. I have a two-level house that I bought so that I could live in the lower level and rent out the upper level. Gary had been wanting us to move in together even before he lost his apartment—"

"But you hadn't said yes to it."

"Not quite," Maicy hedged, though the truth was she had not been sure she was ready for that. "But between not wanting him to move back to Montana and the need for him to find another place—"

"You caved and let him move in."

"It wasn't caving, really..." Although it actually had been. "Gary has worked construction, too, so he offered to do the upstairs remodel for me—which saved me a lot of money. And he did a nice job."

She was torn—she had cause to be bitter and angry at her almost-husband and that made her disinclined to say anything good about him. But she also didn't want Conor to think she'd been about to marry someone who was a lesser man.

"And then you just decided to get married?" Conor asked.

"He proposed about three months ago."

"Without a job, living off you in your place?"

"He was at a low point," she said with some impatience of her own because she could hardly deny what was the truth. "But he said he loved me and that even though he didn't have much to offer, he was hopeful that he'd rebound and he wanted to take the first positive step by asking me to marry him. *He* asked *me*," she finished pointedly.

"And it would have been kicking him when he was down to say no."

Yes.

Instead of saying that, Maicy said, "And I knew how awful it was to propose and be rejected. Especially how awful it was to be in the middle of a really bad time and—"

"Okay, I have that coming," Conor said to stop her.

"And I loved Gary," she went on anyway. "Maybe not with all that teenage obsession—"

Something she hadn't felt since she *was* a teenager. Something she'd only ever felt for Conor...

"—but I loved him in a comfortable way that can make for a good, content, companionable, life-long marriage," she continued. "I want a family and so did he, and he was a good candidate for that, too. I didn't think there would be any *surprises*—" She said that word as if it were a curse. "Better a rational, mature, thinking-person's choice than teenage heat of passion that lets you down!"

So much for being the cooler head...

But all Conor said was, "So you said yes."

Maicy took a deep breath, wishing again that she hadn't shown so much emotion.

"So I said yes," she confirmed more calmly. "We were going to get married in Northbridge because that's where Gary's family is. The only person I really cared about being there was my friend Rachel—"

"Who made the cake."

"But after she'd said she'd be my matron of honor and do the cake—she's a pastry chef—she got pregnant and couldn't travel. So she just made the cake and arranged for a bakery in Northbridge to assemble it when I got it there."

"I only found that one little box," Conor pointed out.

"That's because the rest of the tiers are at the

church, put together by the person the local bakery sent—Candace. But before she got to the top tier, she got to Gary."

And that was when her anger and hurt returned to her voice. To her.

They'd finished eating and Conor sat back and angled in her direction. Maicy slumped back, but stayed facing straight ahead to avoid looking at Conor.

"What do you mean *she got to Gary*?" he asked kindly.

"I was dressed and ready for the photographer to take the pre-wedding pictures in front of the church. On our way outside, we had to go through the room in the church basement where the reception was going to be. And there it all was—three layers of cake looking beautiful and Gary kissing Candace."

"Ohh, Maicy…" Conor said sympathetically.

"The poor photographer froze. She didn't know what to do. But I did. I knew there was no way I was marrying him! So I grabbed that last bakery box—because I wasn't going to leave *all* of Rachel's hard work for those jerks—I grabbed my purse and my suitcase, and I got out of there!"

"And where were you going in this snow?"

A reasonable question that didn't have a reasonable answer.

"All I could think about was getting as far away from Gary and Northbridge as I could. I headed toward Denver, not thinking about the weather or…or really anything but getting away. I didn't even notice that the weather was bad—although now that I look back, I don't think it was quite as bad yet in Northbridge when I left. I just kind of drove into the storm as it was coming. And then the deer appeared out of nowhere and I hit the brakes and... That's it. The next thing I knew I was waking up here."

She could feel his eyes on her and she finally glanced over at him, finding him watching her, his eyebrows arched and an expression a little like the photographer's had been.

"I don't know what to say... I mean, there are a lot of things I *want* to say, but—"

"Go ahead," she dared him, "tell me that's what I get for not being as strong as you were, not being strong enough to say no when he proposed because maybe I didn't really love him, and because he was another guy who probably didn't really love me. Go ahead and tell me that I was his rebound that he ditched when one look at his old girlfriend sent him running to her. Go ahead and tell me that if I'd really loved him I wouldn't have been half-glad to find them that way or feel relieved that I didn't end up having to marry him," she said, once again blurting out more than she probably should have.

"I was *not* going to say any of *that*!" he protested, taking a turn at being defensive.

Then he sighed and said, "I have no right to judge your relationship with Gary. But when it comes to us... nothing you're laying at my door is—"

Right. As if he really *had* loved her but bailed on her anyway.

"All I'll say about Gary," he said, "is that you deserve so much better than that—because you do. I can tell you that I think you *should* be relieved because you dodged a bullet not marrying some guy who should have gotten his act together before he ever proposed.

A guy who should have been out pounding on every door to get a job, not playing Mr. Fix-it while *you* were trying to do that *for* him. A guy who did you a favor by showing his colors *before* the wedding—"

"You'd like Rachel, you think alike," Maicy muttered since she knew those were things her friend would also have said. Rachel had been a little leery of Gary all along and suggested that, if nothing else, maybe the wedding shouldn't happen until after he was employed again.

Conor sighed a second time and Maicy peripherally saw him shake his head. "Sorry," he said. "It isn't easy for me to hear about you with some other guy. I should just be supportive and understanding. You're probably hurt and—"

Maicy made a face and shook her head. "I'm really not, that's the thing... I mean not..." Not the way she'd hurt when Conor had rejected her. But she wasn't going to confess to *that*! "I know it probably says something rotten about me, but I do keep feeling like I dodged a bullet. And then feeling guilty for that."

"What I think is that that's *your* gut talking to you the way mine was yesterday when it sounded to me like Declan was a little off and it crossed my mind to get back to him instead of coming here. *Something* was wrong with you and Gary, and deep down you know it's just better that you didn't get to the altar."

That was putting everything in a nutshell but it helped more than he could know to think that her relief was coming purely from instinct. And not because of the issues Drake—the man she'd been involved with before Gary—had accused her of. She really didn't want to end up dying alone someday—the destiny

Drake had so ominously predicted as the result of her independence...

"I hope you're right," she said, sitting up once more to stack their bowls and plates to take to the kitchen.

Conor stood and followed her. "And now we have cake!" he said, clearly forcing cheerfulness into the mix in an attempt to lighten the mood.

Maicy laughed at his attempt and that helped, too. "Just show me whatever tricks need to be used to wash these dishes," she mock-grumbled.

He took over, using the same tactics for dishwashing that they had to use for showering—water on only as needed—while Maicy dried them, ignoring his orders to sit down and let him do the cleanup.

When the pot, pan and dishes were finished and put away, Maicy opened the cake box.

But cake wasn't the only thing inside. The cake topper was there, too. A groom carrying a bride he was kissing.

And that gave her pangs.

The trouble was, the pangs weren't over Gary. The groom was too tall-seeming, too brawny and broad-shouldered to resemble her former fiancé and instead looked to her like Conor.

Conor who—even though she hadn't been aware of it yesterday—must have carried her over the threshold like that groom was carrying his bride.

Conor who, once upon a time, had kissed her like that groom was kissing his bride.

Conor who had kissed her like no one since...

She swallowed hard and pushed even harder on those memories and the absolutely stupid urges they triggered for him to kiss her like that again...

Absolutely stupid! she silently shouted at herself.

And of course she wouldn't let that happen. Even if he was so inclined. Which she knew he wasn't.

"You know, on second thought, I don't feel like cake. I think I'm just going to go to bed," she said then, feeling defeated by so many things but most of all by her inability to stop thinking about kissing Conor.

"Are you okay? How's your head?" he asked with low-grade alarm.

"I'm just tired," she insisted. "I probably should have done more resting than I did today. Like you told me to. But feel free to have cake if you feel like it."

"I'll wait," he said.

Maicy took the topper out of the box and dropped it unceremoniously into the trash bag before she closed the lid on the cake.

Then she glanced up and caught Conor watching her, taking it all in, a softness and compassion in his blue eyes.

"I think you did the right thing by running out on that wedding before it could happen," he said, that deep voice of his quiet, soothing. "You really do deserve better."

She merely shrugged, appreciating his words but wishing they were being said by anyone else.

Then he said, "I won't wake you the way I did last night, so you don't have to leave your door open. But I will keep the fire burning—somebody was smart to build that thing so it opens into both rooms."

"I can sleep but you aren't going to?" she asked.

"Doctors get pretty used to interrupted sleep so it isn't any big deal. After a lot of years of it, I can wake up instantly and go back to sleep the same way, the minute my head hits the pillow again. I just won't bother you when I do it."

Maicy merely nodded and said good-night, escaping into the bedroom.

But those uninvited thoughts of kissing him went with her.

And she ended up feeling as if she and Conor were still too close for comfort.

Chapter Four

By Tuesday the snow total went up and so did Conor's stress level. He still couldn't get a cell phone signal anywhere near the cabin.

To make matters worse, the roof had begun to groan under the weight of the snow accumulated up there. When he'd gone up the ladder to take a look, he'd discovered dangerously deep drifts.

He knew that put the roof at risk of caving in so rather than heading away from the cabin in search of a signal as he'd intended, he had to stay and deal with that.

At least the hard physical labor of shoveling the snow off the roof helped the tension. And today he needed that on two counts.

With the development of sepsis, a patient like Declan could go into multiple organ failure in the blink of an eye and it had been twenty-four hours since he'd been able to make any contact with his brother's doctor. Twenty-four hours during which anything—the worst—could have happened.

"You better be fighting like hell even without me, D," he said as he shoveled snow off the roof, as if his message would somehow get to Declan through the cosmos.

Then he reminded himself of the things Maicy had emphasized for him the night before—that both he and Declan had made Declan's allergies widely known; that Vince Collier was a good man, a good doctor who covered all the bases; that there was the possibility that everyone treating Declan might be inspired to put a little extra effort into his brother's care because they knew Conor was a navy doctor and that Declan was a decorated marine.

He just had to hang on to hope. But Conor was still so worried it was eating him alive and hard physical labor was the only thing keeping him sane.

Well, not the only thing.

It had, after all, been Maicy who had pointed out the very things he was using to get a grip. That meant she had a hand in his sanity, too.

He was grateful for her injecting some reason into his out-of-control worries.

Now that he thought about it, he was also grateful not to be here alone with those worries. To have someone to vent them to. Someone to distract him from them. He couldn't imagine how much worse this would be if he was alone up here.

On the other hand, Maicy being here was the second reason he needed the hard physical labor to distract him from his frustration and guilt—and other feelings he didn't want to think about…

She hadn't forgiven him—that seemed to be getting clearer and clearer. Not that he deserved it, because he didn't. But over the years he'd hoped—that damn word again—that maybe she had.

Instead, when she'd had that spontaneous outpouring last night, he'd realized that far from being forgiven, his actions had twisted in her mind into something far worse than they'd truly been.

As if it hadn't been bad enough.

And if that warped version was what she'd taken away and carried around with her since she was seventeen, it only compounded things.

They were going to have to talk about it, he realized.

He didn't want to. It was opening an old wound that he wished would just finish healing already. But the longer they were here, the more clear it became to him that healing wouldn't happen until they resolved things between them.

He'd hoped he might use this time in the cabin to mend fences. But now he saw that he needed to be making corrections, too, and he couldn't go on putting it off. Because if she thought what she seemed to think, she was wrong.

Or was he the one who was wrong?

He'd assumed when she'd made that remark about Gary being *another* guy who hadn't really loved her that she'd been referring to him not loving her eighteen years ago. There wasn't a third guy, was there? Someone other than him—and now Gary—who had hurt her, too?

God, he hoped not.

She really—*really*—didn't deserve that. What he'd done was bad enough. He couldn't stand the thought that anyone else had come along and caused her equal amounts of pain. Let alone that there might have been two to follow in his footsteps.

Of course he didn't want to think there had been anyone who had followed him with her, period, he admitted.

Maicy with another guy? *Any* other guy? Ever? Yeah, he hadn't let his mind go there.

Even the whole wedding dress thing—he'd only been able to handle the idea of her all dressed up to marry someone else by convincing himself that she'd run away from her wedding because the guy she'd been about to marry hadn't lived up to him.

He knew that was self-centered and arrogant. But it was the sole way he *could* think about her on the verge of marrying another guy. And she hadn't seemed too upset about the aborted wedding so that had fed his delusions.

But what topped the strain of thinking about her with someone else, was thinking about someone—or multiple someones—hurting her. It was harder even than knowing he had. Because at least he'd had good intentions.

As if that mattered.

Or had made any of it any easier.

And God, nothing about it had been easy...

That first year he'd been away at college, that first year after he'd left her, it was a miracle that he'd passed his classes and kept up with the training and demands of his ROTC scholarship. His head—his heart—had still been back in Northbridge. With Maicy.

For months he'd called home every day—sometimes two and three times a day—asking anyone who answered the phone how she was doing. Until his family had taken a hard line with him and refused to talk about her.

She's going to school and doing what she's supposed to be doing, and that's what you need to be doing, too. So stop this and get on with it! his stepfather had said sternly before telling him that no one would talk to him about Maicy from then on—he'd made it a house rule.

Only his mother hadn't strictly adhered to it. She'd tossed him a crumb of information about Maicy here and there after that. Not much, but enough to reassure him that Maicy was all right, that she was doing fine without him.

And as much as it had ripped him apart to consider that she might have just forgotten about him, he'd also told himself—and known—that it was for the best if she had.

It was just that he hadn't been able to stand the thought of other guys being included in that moving on.

But the possibility that she might think that he'd rejected her proposal years ago because he hadn't loved her? That was not something that had ever occurred to him. And that did make the situation worse.

They were definitely going to have to talk about it. He couldn't let her go on believing that, especially if the misinterpretation might be still influencing anything in her life.

So they were going to have to talk about the past.

While he contended with the present...

He'd been through the navy's toughest training. He'd been through military conflicts. He'd been stationed on an aircraft carrier and a submarine and in some of the harshest conditions the Middle East had to offer.

And nothing had been as hard as facing the fact that he and Maicy were a long—*long*—way from how they'd been years and years ago.

It wasn't as if he hadn't resolved his feelings for her. It was just that sometimes, alone in this cabin, he looked at her and it was like he was a kid again. As if they'd just suffered through a summer apart and now they were together again.

A summer apart, not eighteen years.

And he just wanted to grab her and pull her into his arms and kiss her hello…

It was crazy. And of course he'd never do it. But the inclination was there.

Maybe more than an inclination.

Because last night he'd been watching when she'd opened the box with her wedding cake in it. He'd seen her staring at that wedding topper, seen her throw it away.

And while he didn't know what was going on in her head, he'd had to think that regardless of what she'd said about being relieved not to marry Gary Stern, some not-pleasant emotions had struck her. And he'd had to fight to do nothing to comfort her.

He'd had to fight against the damned biggest urge to hold her and have her face against his chest and her body against his…

He took a particularly large shovelful of snow and threw it from the roof with a vengeance.

No, *that* would not go into the talk they needed to have.

Whatever feelings he might still have for her, he sure as hell wouldn't act on them.

Couldn't act on them.

Because they weren't kids anymore and they hadn't just spent a summer apart. And even if she knew where she was going from here, he wasn't so sure about his own future, and to start anything up with her now wouldn't be any better than what Gary Stern had done.

So he'd just keep shoveling snow, he told himself. He'd just keep trying to get through to the hospital and Declan and Declan's doctor, and using hard physical labor to keep everything contained.

Everything including keeping his hands to himself.

But he and Maicy did need to talk. Like it or not.

And he was going to make sure they did.

After witnessing three dizzy spells that had forced Maicy to grab for the nearest thing to keep herself from falling, Conor had given her even more strict orders to rest.

And so, reluctantly, Maicy had spent Tuesday on the couch, curled up with the magazines and the book she'd packed for her honeymoon, trying not to think about the fact that she was essentially in Conor's bed.

The couch was, after all, where he slept. And even though his bedding was neatly folded, stacked and out of the way, Maicy couldn't stop herself from imagining him lying exactly where she was. Picturing him here, his big body stretched out in all its male glory, set off thoughts and unwelcome memories.

The last Fourth of July that they'd been together they'd gone into a park in Northbridge to watch fireworks. Conor had found them the perfect spot and they'd spread a blanket under a huge oak tree. He'd sat with his back against that tree and become her chair, pulling her to sit between his legs, his arms wrapped around her.

And even though nearly two decades had passed since then, sitting on that sofa where he slept, the L of the sofa's back and side wrapped around her the way he had been that night, she couldn't escape reliving the way that had felt. They'd fit together so impeccably that it had seemed natural and right and the way it would always be.

And she couldn't help wondering how it would feel if he was there on the couch with her, sitting like that again now. Wondering if they would still fit...

Just read! she commanded herself, trying for the umpteenth time to concentrate on her book. But she only made it about two sentences further before her mind wandered back to Conor.

The rhythmic sound of his shoveling, which came from up on the roof, was soothing. A mental picture of him all bundled up, all muscle underneath the snow gear...

She growled at herself when she realized she was doing it again. Thinking about him again.

He was like a song she couldn't get out of her head.

Of course a song playing over and over in her head didn't mean anything, she reasoned. It didn't even mean she liked the song—in fact, more often than not, it was a song she *didn't* like. It was just a weird, glitchy annoyance. Something that happened for no reason, against her will, that she couldn't stop. That meant absolutely nothing.

Thinking about Conor fell into that category, she told herself. And it didn't mean anything, either.

But she really wished it would stop. It served no

purpose at all—except to irritate her. Bad enough that they were stuck here, in these close quarters, alone together. Not having a minute of peace from thoughts of him, from memories of him, from images of him, only made it worse.

She wiggled around to try to shake him out of her brain just as a fast movement of something outside caught her eye.

She glanced through the window over the couch, thinking that it had probably been a clump of snow falling from the porch overhang or a nearby tree.

Instead what she saw caused her to sit up straighter in alarm.

"Uh-oh!"

The movement had been a mountain lion jumping from the elevation of the piled-up snow onto the top of Conor's SUV.

A mountain lion that looked very interested in the activity on the roof.

The roof that the cat could easily reach from the vehicle it was perched on.

"Oh jeez… Are you seeing this, Conor?" she wondered out loud.

The sound of him working didn't stop so she had to assume he wasn't aware that a cougar was eyeing him like he was its evening meal.

She knew that Conor had gone up the ladder from the back side of the cabin, that that was where the ladder still was. If only he'd see the cat, he could climb down and get inside.

But she just kept hearing the sounds of his shovel scraping the shingles, the snow thrown off and hitting the ground over and over again.

And the cat was in hunting mode—statue-still, waiting, gauging, definitely not calling any more attention to itself.

Should she go out the rear door and shout for Conor to come in? Warn him?

Or would any change in what he was doing prompt the animal to strike? With the way the cat was watching him, she didn't think she had much time. She had to do *something* before it pounced!

She'd grown up in Northbridge—a rural town surrounded by open countryside. Wild animal sightings weren't unheard of. She tried to recall what was supposed to be done when faced with one. Play dead? Get away as fast as possible? Make noise and commotion and *not* run because that would prompt the animal to chase?

Which scenario was best for this?

She wasn't sure.

The lion tilted back ever so slightly and raised its head, surveying, just waiting for its moment.

There was no time to warn Conor.

Scaredy-cat...

It was a dumb thing to go through her mind but she decided to take it as a cue for the right choice of response—scare the cat away.

Afraid that pounding on the window might not be enough, she ran to the kitchen, grabbed a metal pot and a wooden spoon and ran back to the cabin's door. She could still keep an eye on the cat from there.

Not wanting to make herself a target, either, she only opened the door a crack, keeping her knee on the back of it so she could slam it closed if the lion's attention turned to her.

Then she started banging with all her might on the bottom of the pan and shouting at the top of her lungs, "Shoo! Shoo! Shoo! Get out of here! Shoo!"

Startled, the cat made a quick pivot, leaped off the SUV and ran into the woods.

"Oh, thank God!" Maicy muttered to herself while her heart went on racing. Dizziness hit her again and as she closed the door she rested her forehead to it, waiting for the spinning to stop.

That was when it occurred to her that the sounds of Conor's rooftop snow shoveling had stopped.

Then she heard him call, "Thanks," before he went back to work.

"I hope the look on your face means that you couldn't get a cell phone signal on the roof," Maicy said when Conor came in an hour later, after dark. One glance at those chiseled features told her he wasn't happy. "Or did you get through and get bad news about Declan?"

"No signal," Conor answered dourly.

"You know the saying—no news is good news..." Maicy offered.

"Not sure that applies here," he grumbled.

"I know. I also know it probably doesn't matter, but for what it's worth, I'm trying to stay positive."

He'd shed his outerwear and was setting it in front of the fire to dry again, so there was a moment before he said, "Declan needs a whole lot more than positive thinking to help him, but it's good for me. It also helps to come in here and see you and get out of my head a little bit and know I'm not in it alone." Then he left the room to take a shower.

Like the night before, though, the shower seemed to

lessen some of his tension. When he returned—again looking better than he should in his sweatsuit—he was in slightly improved spirits.

As he heated canned spaghetti he asked how she felt and how much dizziness she'd had while he was outside.

"Not as much as before," she assured him.

But still he refused to let her get up to help and brought everything to her.

As he settled on the couch, he actually laughed before he said, "*Shoo*? To a *mountain lion*?"

Maicy glanced at him over her shoulder. When they were teenagers and he'd laughed or smiled, lines hadn't been drawn at the corners of his eyes the way they were now. But they somehow accentuated those eyes, and Maicy judged the lines a nice addition.

"Did you see the cat before that—because I could still hear you shoveling and I didn't think you had," she asked.

"No, I hadn't seen it. I heard that racket you were making and looked up just as it turned tail and jumped off the car. That was a close call—one leap and it would have had me."

"That did seem to be what it had in mind."

"But *shoo*?" he repeated, laughing again and making her realize that lighter spirits put parentheses on either side of his sensual mouth, too. "Again—who *shoos* a mountain lion?"

"I didn't know what else to do. Did you want me to just let it get you?" Maicy asked.

He laughed again, this time wryly. "It probably would have given you some satisfaction if it had. So thanks for not giving in to that and saving my ass."

"Now we're even…for you hauling me out of my car so I didn't freeze to death."

That sobered his expression and arched his full eyebrows. "But nothing evens the score for all those years ago when you needed me to save you and I didn't," he said as if filling in the rest. "I wanted to talk about that…"

"There's nothing to talk about. It was what it was." A rejection from the only other person she'd trusted besides her mother. "But just to be clear," she added, "I wasn't asking you to save my life back then. Just to move up the schedule."

After dating for nearly three years and falling in love with him, believing him when he'd told her they'd have a future together, she'd turned to him instinctively when her mother had been in a fatal car accident just before the start of her senior year of high school.

No one had heard from her father in four years, and there hadn't been any other family. Maicy had been left with her mother's small bank account, only the remainder of the month to stay in their apartment and nothing besides the income from her part-time job at the ice cream parlor to live on.

"I was just asking you to marry me *ahead* of the schedule we'd already planned," she reiterated.

"I know. But—"

"You didn't want to," she said flatly.

"It wasn't that, Maicy. You know how it was—I was going to college on an ROTC scholarship *and* an accelerated program that combined college and medical school into six years. That meant a heavy course load along with ROTC training and obligations. We were supposed to do things long-distance until you graduated college and *then* get married—"

"But things had changed, and colleges have housing for married students," she said in a calm, reasonable tone that was nothing like the frantic, desperate, scared way she'd said it to him long ago when she'd begged him to marry her before he left so she could go with him.

"It was so much more complicated than that," he responded. "I was leaving in two weeks, but I wasn't going to turn eighteen for two more months and there was no way my mom or Hugh would sign permission. It was too late to arrange for couples' housing and under the terms of my scholarship, I was required to live on campus. Even if something had opened up at the last minute in married housing, my scholarship wouldn't have covered it—we would have had to come up with rent money. And on top of all that, you still had a year left of high school—I didn't want to risk you not graduating. Even if you'd tried finishing school in Missouri, would you really have been able to pull it off? Married, trying to work to earn our rent money and commuting to a high school without a car? With me needing to study as much as I knew I would have to—as much as I *did* have to? With me not having a minute to spare for you? For us?"

He'd finished his spaghetti and set the bowl on the coffee table before he leveled those piercing blue eyes at her and went on. "You were upset about your mom, in a panic…anyone in that situation would have been. But you weren't thinking clearly and I *had* to. I had to make sure all the bases were covered for us both—"

"Like you did for your own mother. And for your

brothers and sister and the farm when your mom bottomed out when you were a little kid."

"Yeah, it *was* like that! You weren't thinking any straighter than my mom was then. Again, I understood, it was an emotional time for you—"

"But not for you," she accused.

"Yes, for me, too!"

"But not nearly enough for you to actually go through with what we'd talked about and get married."

"Because neither of us was ready to get married, no matter what our feelings were," he said gruffly. "And that's exactly what I wanted to talk about. That remark you made last night that Gary was *another* guy who probably didn't love you. You don't really think that, do you? That I didn't love you? Come on…" he chastised a second time in disbelief.

Disbelief? Really? He was really that surprised that she'd gotten the message that he didn't love her? What else was she supposed to think? She'd believed that he'd put them first—that staying together was as important to him as it was to her. But when she'd proposed, he'd just been full of excuses for why she couldn't come with him.

"Then don't go…"

That's what she'd said to him eighteen years ago when they'd had this argument the first time.

And along with rejecting her proposal, he also hadn't chosen the option of staying.

If he'd loved her the way she'd loved him, he would have done one of the two, no matter what it would have taken. When he hadn't, she'd known that he didn't love her the way she'd loved him.

"It's all water under the bridge," she said rather than answer his question.

"You're wrong if you believe that I didn't care," he said earnestly. "I never intended for us to go our separate ways—I just wanted us to stay the course we'd set. Once I knew that arrangements could be made for you to move in with the minister and his wife to be the nanny to their kids while you finished high school, I just wanted us to get back on track. I wanted you to go on to college and graduate, and *then* we could get married the way we'd planned. It was you who broke up with me."

It *had* been her who had broken up with him. Because his refusal to make any change to the plan, to stand by her when her entire life had fallen apart, his choice to leave, smacked of her childhood.

"Yeah, my father always claimed to have *feelings* for my mom and me, but that didn't stop him from bolting at the slightest bump in the road."

"Oh, that's not fair, either! Comparing me to your old man?"

"Actually, as time went on and I got over…things…I gave you points for *not* doing what he did, for not marrying me and *then* running out on the promises that marriage came with. At least you nipped it in the bud before we got married. But it still wasn't what I was counting on from you."

"Ah, Maicy…" he lamented.

"Like I said, water under the bridge."

He took a breath and sighed. "It was a lousy situation at a lousy time."

"For me. It didn't change your life at all. You did what you were set to do—you went to college, became a doctor and joined the navy the way you'd always planned."

"I asked about you... My mom said you were doing okay."

There was some accusation in that that Maicy didn't understand. But it was so ludicrous it made her laugh.

"I was doing okay?" she repeated. "Yeah, I was doing great. That whole year, I did just great," she said sarcastically. "And then I did great the first year of college, too." She refused to confide in him about the days when she hadn't been able to get out of bed, or when she barely went through the motions, overwhelmed by more tears than she'd thought she was capable of producing, feeling as if she was in such a deep, dark hole that she might not ever get out of it.

"My mother was just trying to make me feel better by telling me you were okay," he said as if he'd always feared that might be the case.

Maicy didn't think she needed to confirm it. Instead she said somewhat defiantly. "I did learn not to depend on anyone—that's a good thing. When I imagine the person I might have been had you *not* left me hanging I'd rather be who I am now."

Conor was staring at her, scrutinizing her, and she didn't like that so she stood, took his bowl and hers and went to the kitchen with them.

He followed her with the box of crackers, replacing them in the mudroom.

When he joined her as she washed the dirty dishes, he leaned against the counter beside where she stood at the sink, facing the opposite direction, dishtowel in hand, at the ready for drying-duty.

"What would you have ended up being?" he asked then.

"Weak," she answered with more defiance. "Dependent on you instead of being independent." Though that unyielding self-reliance had been what had irked Drake, and her strength had maybe not been the best thing when it came to Gary...

"I guess I might have just been your tagalong rather than my own person," she added. "Or worse, what my mother was—constantly waiting for a man who was off doing his own thing without any regard for her or his kid."

"So I had no love, no *regard* for you. And your mother's lot in life is how you would have ended up if we *had* gotten married," he concluded as she dried her hands on one end of the dishtowel he was using and then took up a stance with her hips against the utility table across from him.

She only raised a challenging chin to his summary.

Finished with his part of the chore he tossed the dishtowel to the counter with some force before he scowled at her. "I had regard for you then and I still do. I've never *not* had *regard* for you."

Maicy shrugged as if it didn't matter. And she wouldn't let it matter because she couldn't really believe him anyway.

He shook his head as if he was shaking something off. Then, in a less agitated tone, said, "What if, Maicy? What if nothing bad had happened to your mom and once we were apart life had just insidiously taken us on separate paths and what we were to each other had just dwindled off the way first love can? Would everything that came before, everything we did and shared, all we had together, still be canceled out? Because we *were* happy together...really happy..."

She wouldn't concede to that and still didn't answer him.

He went on anyway.

"Take away that shadow, Maicy, and that time before, those *years* before, are still the best memories I have, and I can't tell you how much I hate that that isn't true for you. I have moments when I remember something so sweet or nice or funny or…so you…and I can't stand to think that all that's left of that for you is bad."

She closed her eyes tight, fighting, fighting, fighting so hard against it.

But when she opened her eyes again it came out anyway. In a whisper.

"It isn't," she confessed.

"So the ending didn't poison everything that came before," he said quietly, his deep voice even deeper. Standing there tall and straight and strong and so sexy she just wanted to hit him.

But it didn't change anything—not the fact that he'd made her think about how the first snow every year reminded her of when he'd shown up at her door to take her for a midnight walk in it.

Not the fact that he'd made her think about what it had felt like every single time he'd held her hand.

Not the fact that he'd made her think about picnics and country drives and kisses in front of her school locker and how no one had ever been able to make her laugh like he had.

And not the fact that he was now the most gorgeous man she'd ever been in this close a proximity to.

None of it changed anything, she told herself firmly. Because the way they'd ended *had* cast a big black shadow over everything else for her. And she needed not to let that shadow recede.

Especially not when she was locked here in this tiny cabin alone with him, mere days after running out on her wedding to someone else. She needed some serious time and thought put into her future relationships before she ever ventured near another one. Especially with Conor.

So no, she couldn't let anything be changed.

But something else had shifted with that stupid admission that she hadn't forgotten the good because suddenly he took a step that put him in front of her. For a moment, it seemed as if he was going to move the few inches nearer to start kissing her now...

She raised her chin a bit higher in what she convinced herself was more defiance. A dare for him to just try it so she could shoot him down.

But after another minute of whatever it was that was hanging in the air between them, he pulled back, nearly plopped against the counter again, and glanced at the pink box that still held the uncut top of her wedding cake.

"Dessert?" he asked in a voice more jagged than it had been.

Maicy had no idea why she was suddenly struck by a double punch of frustration and disappointment, but it soured her on the idea of cake for a second night.

So she said, "No, saving your ass tired me out—I think I'll just go to bed and read awhile."

He smiled at the *saving his ass* part and nodded. "I do want you to get rest."

"Good night then," she said aloofly, heading for the bedroom.

But after stepping into it, before closing the door behind her, she stole another glance at him.

He was still standing there, still watching her.

With an expression on that handsome face that made her think he was reliving something from their past.

The good or the bad? she wondered.

Knowing as she closed the door that even though it was memories of the bad she wanted to take to bed with her, now that he'd made her think of them, it was more likely memories of the good that were going to haunt her tonight.

Chapter Five

Wednesday brought Conor more worry and frustration along with still more snow from that unrelenting storm.

He spent the morning shoveling the porch and the path to the woodpile, and again clearing snow from the cabin's roof and from his rented SUV before letting the vehicle run for ten minutes to keep the battery from dying and to add a little charge to his cell phone.

When he went in to warm up he also heated water for the shower Maicy said she was desperate for since he'd persuaded her to skip one on Tuesday in order to do nothing but rest.

While she was showering, he ate a lunch of dried salami and crackers and tried not to think about Maicy naked and wet just a room away.

When he couldn't stop himself from fantasizing

about joining her, he decided he'd better get out of there.

So he bundled up again to snowshoe away from the cabin in search of cell service, hoping to God he didn't have to go another day without word of his brother.

When he did find a spot where he could get reception and he reached Declan's doctor the news wasn't good.

His brother had had an allergic reaction to one of the combination of antibiotics he'd been given. His blood pressure was alarmingly low, his lung and kidney functions were compromised. And the results of lab tests to isolate the bacteria causing the infection had been delayed because the lab was shorthanded.

"I'm going to the lab myself right now," Vince told him. "And I'm not leaving until I have an answer. I'm sticking with him, Conor, I haven't left the hospital since I got here yesterday morning. You should know that whichever of the antibiotics he reacted to wasn't one on your allergy list—I'm making sure he isn't getting any of those. But apparently there are others he can't take, either. I'm starting him on a new combination now and I'm administering them myself, one at a time, and monitoring him for a reaction so I can be sure he can tolerate them. We're doing our best for him."

Conor knew the warning tone in the other doctor's voice because he'd used it himself too often—it was the implied *but* that meant that despite doing his best for Declan, Declan was getting worse.

"I need to be there!" Conor said through clenched teeth.

"Believe me, I wish you were—for Declan's sake and because I could use the help," said the other doctor, who sounded as tired and overworked as Conor knew he was. "But I promise you I'm doing everything I can."

"I know, I know. And I'm just keeping you from it," Conor said, trying to be patient when he was anything but. Then he said, "Any chance I can talk to Declan?"

"I have him heavily sedated."

So no.

As much as Conor didn't want to cut off the connection once he had it, he knew Declan needed Vince's attention more than he did so he let the call end. Then, fighting hard against the out-of-control feelings his helplessness sent through him, he forced himself to refocus, sent the text Maicy had asked him to send to her friend Rachel if he found service, and—since he still had reception—called Rickie in Northbridge.

Unfortunately, Rickie still couldn't give him a timetable for when he might be able to escape the small town to plow the road up to the cabin in order for Conor and Maicy to get out.

Rickie also informed him that there were even more road closures and that there wasn't an airport in all of Montana open, dashing any hope at all that Conor could get back to Declan anytime soon.

So with his stress level at the limit, Conor returned to the cabin and took it out in splitting more wood.

And somehow, somewhere along the way, he went from worrying about Declan to thinking about his conversation with Maicy the night before.

She really was holding one hell of a grudge against him. And even after all these years, she still didn't see things the way he had.

But she *was* right that he'd gone into a mode similar to what he'd had to do as a kid when his mother had bottomed out—something he'd told Maicy about when they were dating.

He'd been seven years old when it happened for no reason he'd understood at the time. One afternoon, a few months before Kinsey was born, they'd come home from school and she'd been sobbing at the kitchen table over a newspaper article about a plane crash. The plane crash that he'd learned later had taken the life of his mother's *friend* Mitchum Camden.

After that there was a long period when his mother hadn't gotten out of bed, when she'd just stayed there crying. It had been up to him to get breakfast, fix school lunches, to get himself and the twins dressed and onto the bus that would take them all to the school where he was in the second grade and where the twins went to preschool.

Days and then weeks and then months when his mother had left it up to him to fix dinner, to give his brothers a bath and put them to bed at night. She'd managed to give him instructions on what to tell Smith— the man who ran the farm for them—but she wouldn't leave her bed to see her orders carried out, which left it up to him. Conor had to be *the man of the house*, his mother had told him.

He'd been scared. Confused. Worried, too, because he hadn't known what had happened to change his usually cheery, caring mother. But he'd taken the responsibility she'd placed on him seriously. And he'd begun to map out how to take care of everything that needed to be done.

He'd learned that if he planned ahead and stuck to

his plan, to his schedule, he could make sure Declan, Liam and his mother were taken care of.

He'd learned to be the intermediary between the rest of the world and his mother—who had lost the desire to leave her room even when she did start getting out of bed every day.

He'd learned the importance of organization—even though he didn't know that word—and had made sure lunches were packed the night before for himself and his brothers, made sure they got up on time in the mornings, had breakfast, left the house and never missed the bus that would take them into town.

He'd learned to solve problems that arose—how to stand on a chair brought to the front of the washing machine to do the laundry, how to use that same chair to put away the groceries his mother ordered and had delivered.

He'd become his mother's courier, distributing the checks she wrote for the farmhands on payday, bringing her the mail, putting the checks she wrote to pay the bills out in the box.

He'd kept everything and everyone going until months later when Kinsey had been born and his mother had seemed to come out of her funk.

But even after the burden of looking after his family and the farm were finally taken off his small shoulders, Conor was never the same. He'd been left with a strong sense of responsibility and the need to do everything he could to try to prevent bad things from happening, to take every possible disaster into account and plan accordingly.

He'd become a cautious kid who grew into a cautious teenager, and then a cautious adult, a cautious physician.

So yes, when Maicy's mom had died so unexpectedly and Maicy had been left in a state of panic, both his sense of responsibility and his need for careful restraint had kicked in.

He'd felt responsible for making sure Maicy didn't go off the rails. Responsible for making calm, rational decisions for both of them when she couldn't. Which, to him, meant sticking to their plan in order to make sure that she finished high school and they both got through college before marrying. He'd been convinced that it was his job to keep them both on course the same way he'd kept his family on course when he was seven.

And if he looked at where he and Maicy had gotten in their lives, he thought a case could be made for him having been right. Maicy *had* finished high school, gone on to college and an advanced degree, started her own business. And he'd accomplished what he'd set out to accomplish, too. If he'd given in to her proposal, who knows what might have happened? Even she admitted that she preferred the person she was now to the person she might have become.

But still she resented him for having said no.

Could he use this time together to get her to let go of that grudge?

He really wanted to see that happen.

And the day *was* at an end, he thought, his spirits bouncing back at that prospect.

Without cell service again, he was once more cut off from the outside world, leaving nothing but going inside for an evening with Maicy. And the opportunity to possibly gain a little more ground against that grudge seemed like a worthwhile way to spend that time.

Who are you trying to kid? he asked himself as he finished splitting logs and loaded them into the sling.

Yes, he was again grateful that being with Maicy would offer a distraction from his troubles, and yes, he was glad to have more chance to work on her lingering ill will against him.

But that wasn't the real reason he was eager to go inside. Despite her resentment, he was still looking forward to just being with her. To talking to her. Like in the old days.

He recognized that thinking like that now was a little crazy. These definitely were not the *old days*. And whether or not he broke through the barrier that had risen between them, they'd still walk away from this as two people who shared a past with a bad ending, forced together by circumstances until they were finally able to go their separate ways.

But he'd meant what he'd said when he'd told her that the memories of their past *before* that bad ending were the best he had. And what he hadn't told her was just how often he still revisited those memories. His memories of her.

Memories that had hit him so hard last night that for just a minute he was back with her under the bleachers. Back to when she was his girl and it had been killing him that she was hanging onto her virginity. Back to when he'd at least been able to kiss her.

And he'd wanted to kiss her so much at that moment that it had pushed him to close the distance between them in the kitchen...

Before he'd snapped out of it.

But still it had seemed as if the universe had shifted a little all the way around in that moment. As if it had been okay that he'd gotten that close. As if just maybe, when she'd looked up at him, she hadn't despised him.

And as stupid as it seemed, that split second felt encouraging to him. It had him looking forward to spending the evening with her as more than merely a distraction or a chance to work on her grievance.

There was some danger in that, he told himself.

Because remember there's nowhere for anything to go from here.

But even knowing that was true, he couldn't stop the feeling of urgency to get inside and have this time with her.

And while he'd successfully kept himself busy and away from the cabin all day, now that night was upon them, he could finally give in to it.

Wednesday was the first day that Maicy felt reasonably well again. She only had a slight headache, some periodic dizziness, fewer aches and pains, and less stiffness and weakness. With the exception of the healing cut on her forehead she felt more like herself. And she wanted to look like herself again, too—rather than like a recovering patient.

So even though it used up more water than her first cabin shower had, that afternoon she took a more thorough one with her own bodywash, and she gave herself a far better shampoo, too.

Then, she devoted her afternoon to her appearance. Because the better she looked, the better she felt.

At least that was her reasoning while she tried to

ignore the fact that lurking behind every choice she made were thoughts of Conor.

Conor and what she could do to knock his socks off.

But not to entice him, of course. Only to make him sorry for what he'd passed up. What he'd passed up years ago—and again last night when she'd thought he was going to kiss her. She was tired of being so resistible to him. Especially when it seemed like her own eyes popped out of her head every time she looked at him.

So it was time to get herself back on track.

She was a notorious overpacker and the fact that she'd thought to be spending a few days in wintry Northbridge and returning from her Jamaican honeymoon to also wintry Denver meant that she was equipped for two seasons.

Today she chose a pair of jeans that fit to perfection, and a hunter green, high-neck cashmere sweater that provided the exact amount of accentuation where she wanted it.

Her red hair was thick and naturally wavy, and while she couldn't use her hairdryer, she was careful as she dried it in front of the fire to scrunch it every few minutes. That aided the waves so that it didn't need to be hooked behind her ears or tied up, and could be left loose to fall over her shoulders.

Being a natural redhead, she had the pale porcelain skin to go with it so she never went anywhere without blush and a touch of bronzer to add some color, plus mascara to darken her lashes, so she applied all of that, too.

Standing in front of the mirror in the bedroom, she parted her hair on the side in order for it to camouflage her wound and the two butterfly bandages over it before taking a final assessment.

None-the-worse-for-wear was her verdict.

About how she looked, anyway. But she was reminded that she wasn't at a hundred percent when she realized that her afternoon of beautifying had worn her out.

To deal with that, she rested awhile before turning her attention to dinner.

And to watching, rather impatiently, for Conor to come back.

It was just cabin fever, she told herself. It wasn't that she wanted to see *him*, to spend the evening with *him*. It was just that after hours alone in that quiet, small space with little to do, company—no matter who provided it—became something to break the monotony.

And she decided she was also going to blame thinking about him every minute on cabin fever, boredom and isolation. On not having anyone or anything else *to* think about right now.

And she was going to blame the fact that last night she'd dreamed about him on her head injury.

None of it—not a single minute of any of it—had anything to do with any feelings on her part for the man himself, she assured herself as she kept an eagle eye out the window for him. It didn't matter that he was fantastic-looking or too-sexy-to-believe now. It didn't matter that he had those amazing blue eyes. And it certainly didn't mean that she had any lingering or new attraction to him.

What had been between them was over and done with. And when it became time for her to move on, to date and try to find a new relationship, it would be time to move *on*, not to move backward. To learn from her mistakes—which included him—and use those lessons not to make more mistakes with anyone she let herself get involved with.

The minute she could get out of here Conor would be nothing but history again. Painful, better-forgotten history. And she couldn't wait for that to happen. She couldn't wait to be back in Denver again, to have Rachel to talk to, and to once more put Conor well, well, *well* behind her.

But for the time being, Conor Madison was all she had to counteract the cabin fever, boredom and isolation so he was a necessary evil.

Although even after reassuring herself of all of that, there was just no explanation for why nothing but a necessary evil made her pulse speed up when she heard him return to the cabin.

He didn't come inside right away, though, and she battled disappointment at that. Instead he went around back and began splitting wood behind the house.

But still he was there. And one glimpse of him in all his heavy winter gear just outside gave her a warm rush that she didn't want to acknowledge.

Any more than she wanted to acknowledge the desire to check the mirror to make sure that her hair and makeup were still up to par.

"Look at you!" Conor said when he finally did come inside with the canvas sling filled with wood.

Maicy fought for nonchalance even though it was ridiculously gratifying to hear the admiration in his voice. And even more satisfying to see his gaze go from top to bottom and back again, and to have his eyebrows arch in approval.

"I was tired of convalescent clothes," she said simply.

It must not have fooled him, though, because his eyes went to her hair as if it was the telltale sign of all the effort she'd put into getting ready for tonight.

Or maybe he just liked the way it looked when it was down because he smiled before he went off to heat water and shower while Maicy worked on the evening meal.

Salmon loaf made from canned salmon, cracker crumbs and powdered egg; and mashed potatoes from dried potato flakes.

Maicy thought that this place was the best diet she'd ever been on because she certainly had no desire to overeat.

Conor, on the other hand, ate heartily, assuring her that he'd had worse.

Maicy wondered if it was stress eating when he updated her on how sick Declan was. Conor's even-more-elevated tension and concerns were evident.

Between her inclination to make him feel better and the fact that she was in a stronger frame of mind today, Maicy decided tonight was the night for cake.

Moist, dark chocolate cake with Rachel's delectable buttercream frosting—far superior to what had become common cabin fare.

And it seemed to do the trick for lightening the mood because after taking their slices back to the sofa, where they sat on opposite sides of the couch, each of them angled toward the center, Conor breathed a sigh of satisfaction and said, "Chocolate…if I'd known this wasn't plain old white cake under that frosting this might not still be around. But of course your wedding cake would be chocolate—I should have guessed."

It was an obsession they'd always shared.

"Not just chocolate, *triple* chocolate," Maicy said. "It's a recipe Rachel—who used to own a bakery—makes especially for me so it'll be chocolaty enough."

He tried a bite—savoring it rather than inhaling it the way he had the rest of the meal.

"Now that's good cake," Conor judged. "Too bad you didn't run off with all the tiers."

"I wish I had," Maicy agreed.

"And your friend Rachel couldn't come to the wedding because she's pregnant?"

"After years of fertility treatments and failed attempts to have a baby. Because of her history it's a high-risk pregnancy and her doctor won't let her travel. Otherwise she'd have been my matron of honor."

"And you met Rachel in college?"

"Our first day—we were roommates. Who became more like sisters. She took me home every vacation. Her family sort of adopted me. I spend holidays with them still."

"Nice. I'm glad to hear that," he said sincerely. "And I did send her the text today when I found service, the way you asked. I said I was a friend—I thought that was better than saying I'm your ex. I told her that you're okay but we're snowed in in a cabin near Northbridge. That I have to hike out for cell service and you'll call when you can."

"Oh good! I'm sure she's worrying. That should help. Thanks."

Now that he seemed more relaxed, she felt she

could broach the topic of his worries again. "You told me before that you left Declan because there's been something going on with Kinsey? Is she still in North-bridge?"

"No, she lives in Denver. We were supposed to meet at the farm to start going through Mom and Hugh's things—"

"Your mom and Hugh…" She trailed off with a question in her tone.

"Hugh died not quite two years ago, and then Mom passed in October."

"I'm sorry. I hadn't heard."

"Yeah… Kinsey handled everything—none of us could get home, even for the funerals," he added with regret.

"The navy and the Marines don't let you come back for that?" Maicy said in surprise.

"It depends on where you are, what you're in the middle of. There were different situations for all of us, but both times none of us could swing it. I was on a submarine when Hugh went, and Liam and Declan were in Afghanistan. When it came to Mom…Declan was hurt the day before she died so there was no get-ting back then for Declan or me, and Liam is Special Forces and didn't even get word of it until the funeral was over."

"So poor Kinsey was alone for it all?" Maicy asked.

"Yeah." More guilt was evident in his voice and ex-pression. "It was a lot for her. We all feel rotten about her being stuck with the whole burden, but there was just nothing any of us could do."

"So you came now to make it up to her?"

"No…" he said and there seemed to be some kind

of hedging in the way he said it. "I mean, yeah, we all wish we *could* make it up to her. But I don't think that's possible. And now there's something else to deal with. Something that came out of Mom's death…"

He was clearly reluctant to talk about whatever that something else was, frowning down at his cake, apparently unaware that Maicy was watching him closely, studying him.

Okay, maybe she was drinking in the sight of him.

But he'd come from his shower dressed in jeans and an exceedingly form-fitting heather-gray mockneck T-shirt rather than a sweat suit tonight, and she was only human. The T-shirt molded to every muscle of his torso and it was difficult for her *not* to ogle him.

After a moment of wrestling with his thoughts, he finally said, "When Mom was dying she told Kinsey something…she needed to explain a huge chunk of money we were about to inherit. And then there was a letter, too…"

He hesitated again before he took a deep breath, exhaled with what sounded like resignation, and said, "Mom claims that Mitchum Camden was our biological father."

Maicy had never told Conor that his mother's past was actually one of her own mother's cautionary tales to scare her into maintaining her virginity—a single woman with four bastard children to raise alone, looked down on by some of the town and forced to make ends meet on her own while the father got off scot-free. What her mother hadn't said was who the scot-free father might have been.

"Mitchum Camden," Maicy repeated in genuine shock.

The Camden Superstores, founded decades ago by Northbridge native H.J. Camden when he'd gone to Denver to seek his fortune, had elevated the family to distinction and wealth. The current Camden generation and their grandmother were well respected, but those who had come before had reputations for a slew of dishonorable deeds that had long been swept under the carpet. Apparently including married Mitchum Camden's long-term affair with Alice Shea when he'd frequented the Northbridge ranch that the Camdens owned.

"Did you have any idea before this?" Maicy asked.

Another pause. Another sigh. Before he scrunched up his face and confessed. "I'm the only one of us who's old enough to remember things like my mom's 'friend' who visited us sometimes. And stayed over… He brought us presents and took us outside to play. I didn't know a Camden from a hole in the ground but I knew his name was Mitchum and later, remembering that, I put two and two together." He shook his head. "I've never said that to a soul," he admitted then.

"Not even to Liam or Declan? Not to Kinsey?"

"Not to anyone. Declan and Liam have never said anything to make me think they remember him—and they were only three the last time he was at the farm. Kinsey wasn't even born yet. She was still a baby when Mom met Hugh. From her perspective, he was around from the start. She never had to deal with any growing up without a father's name to protect her. Mom and Hugh got married when Kinsey was two, and after that people were more careful about what they said and they stopped looking at us like we had scales so…" He shrugged those broad shoulders and sighed yet again.

"I liked *not* being a pariah better than being one and kept quiet."

Maicy flinched at that, not having known there was a time when little Conor had felt that way. "How were you a pariah?"

"There were just things… Birthday parties I didn't get invited to and comments about why. Even kids who were my friends at school weren't allowed to come to my house. I'd be in town with my mom and see the looks she got, watch people turn their heads and whisper, snicker. I was too young to really know what it was about, but I knew it was something bad. That they thought *we* were something bad. And I *didn't* know why we didn't have a dad around like everyone else did—something my mom wouldn't talk about even when I asked. It was just obvious that there was something different about us, something other people considered wrong or bad. Then Hugh came on board and things got different."

Hugh Madison had been a retired marine. A big, strapping, ultra-serious man whom no one wanted to cross.

"I guess he made an honest woman out of Mom," Conor went on. "And I was glad to put everything before that out to pasture, to forget about it and be a family like everyone else's. It was dirt I never wanted stirred up again."

"But now?"

"I feel the same way now," he confirmed without a hint of a waver. "As far as I'm concerned, as far as Declan and Liam are concerned, Hugh was our father— he raised us, he was there for us."

"Even if he'd wanted to, Mitchum Camden couldn't

have been there because he was killed in that plane crash with so many of his family," Maicy pointed out.

"Yeah, I know, I picked up the slack when my mom hit bottom after that. But there's nothing in anything he did before to make me think it would have been different even if he had lived. We were his dirty little secret and I'm sure that's what we would have stayed."

"So finding out the truth doesn't change anything for you?"

"Not really. Left to me, I'd go on the way I always have. I'd ignore that piece of the past and only honor what came after it—that Hugh and my mother were our parents, our family. The ones who did right by us. I don't give a damn about the bloodlines."

"But Kinsey does?" Maicy asked.

There was another pause that put chagrin in his expression. "We haven't been there for Kinsey. She's had to carry all the weight here at home. It's cost her friends, relationships… After Mom died, I guess it got to be a really big deal to her that she didn't have anybody. And she started to look at that whole slew of Camdens out there and got these crazy ideas about reaching out to them. Trying to be part of their family so she could have more than three brothers who haven't been there for her. Who aren't there for her. Who she doesn't really have any hope of ever being there for her if we all stay career military."

"But you still don't think she *should* pursue it?" Maicy asked, finishing her cake and setting her plate on the coffee table.

"No matter what we think, she already did it," he said somewhat under his breath. "She brought the letter from our mom to the Camden grandmother."

"Who would also be *your* grandmother—"

"Yeah, that's what Kinsey keeps reminding me."

"How did that go?"

"Not well—it sure as hell didn't go the way Kinsey was hoping it would."

"It went the way you were afraid it might?"

"Well, apparently the grandmother didn't call us bastards and kick her out, but she didn't say *welcome to the family*, either. Seems like Kinsey dropped the bomb and then just had to retreat when the old lady met the news with stony silence. That's how it's been since, except that Kinsey found out that the Camdens hired someone to investigate. I know Kinsey sent them a Christmas card but they didn't send one back."

Maicy had always liked Kinsey Madison and she hated to think of the Camdens or anyone else hurting her feelings. "Poor Kinsey," she said, looking closely at Conor, thinking about him in comparison to the Camdens.

From the publicity pictures she'd seen, there was a resemblance. He did have similar dark, swarthy good looks, although she thought he was even better-looking. But it was the eyes that sold it—the Camden blue eyes. Only with those silvery streaks added to them to make them even more distinctive.

"Anyway," he said, "that's why I came—so maybe I could talk my sister into letting it lie. Especially now because she's gotten engaged and won't be alone anymore."

The way he said that made her think of something else he'd said earlier. "Before, when you said none of you were there for Kinsey and wouldn't be *if* you all stay in the military—is there a chance that any of you won't? That she might have one of you home, too?"

There was another pause, this one longer, before he finished his cake and set the plate on top of Maicy's on the coffee table.

"I don't know... I guess Kinsey isn't the only one of us going through some stuff. I've been kind of...unsettled lately. And I'm up for promotion and if I need to make a change now's the time—it wouldn't be right to take the promotion and then get out."

"What? You mean one of Hugh's recruits might not stay in the military until retirement?" she goaded mildly. Back in the day, she really had been a little resentful of the way that Hugh had pushed all the boys into the idea that they needed to join the military. Conor always swore it was what he wanted, what they all wanted, but she had her doubts. From what Conor had said about his childhood before his mom got married, it was easy to see why he'd practically hero-worshipped his stepfather. The thought of disappointing him would have been a powerful motivation to fall in line with Hugh's plans.

"Believe me, that's part of what makes it tough. I know he'd turn over in his grave if he knew. He might even haunt me," Conor joked.

Maicy was glad to see the lighter side of him still there tonight even though it was waffling with the more serious subjects.

"It isn't the possibility of a haunting that makes this tough on you," she said then. "It's that you need to stick to your plan and if you're starting to doubt the path you're on that's a *huge* deal for you."

"You know me too well, is what you're saying," he said wryly.

Maicy merely challenged him to deny it, with the arch of her eyebrows.

"Yeah, I'll admit that. It goes against my grain. Bigtime. Tell me it serves me right."

Just a little...

But she didn't say that. Instead she said, "You could just make another plan."

He made a sound that was something like a growl. "And you always say that as if it's nothing."

Maicy shrugged. "I counsel a lot of people making job changes. It *is* hard. But it *can* be done."

"It's more complicated for me—and not just because everything in me tells me to stick to the current plan," he insisted.

"Everybody thinks that," Maicy said.

"That doesn't stop it from being true. When I went through rotations in med school I liked being that first guy to help traumatically injured patients—that's why I picked my specialty. Plus I was willing to be stationed overseas, in the thick of any conflict. But as time's gone on I've started not liking that I just patch people up to ship them off, that I don't know if they're getting the care they need afterward. And on top of that I've been hearing about the troubles with the VA hospitals—where my patients need to go when they come home. Now, being with Declan, I've seen for myself the holes in the system those military men and women could easily fall through and that there's cause for concern. But for me to change what I do is—"

"I know, it isn't easy," Maicy sympathized.

"Particularly for people who've had my kind of education and training. In order for me to practice another kind of medicine, it means another residency—that's not going back to square one but almost. The navy has what it paid for in my education. A do-over is not really an option. To make a change, not only would I have to go in reverse, I'd have to leave the navy to do it," he concluded.

"Okay, you're right, your situation is more complicated than most," she allowed. "But what if you separate the two things? If you were a civilian would you stay the course or take the do-over?" she asked.

He frowned. "I guess I never thought about it like that. Separate them, huh? Take the military out of the equation and only focus on the job? *Then* figure out if that's important enough to leave the navy…" he mused.

"Knowing the one might help you make the decision about the other."

"Hmm… I'm gonna have to think about that," he said as if it were a revelation.

Since he seemed to be swimming around in the idea, Maicy opted to leave him to it and took their dessert dishes to the sink to wash. When she'd finished that and turned back to Conor he was in front of the fire, poking at it with the stoker, making room to add wood to the flames.

As so often happened, she was stalled for a moment as her gaze stuck to him. The last couple of hours of being with him and talking as easily as they always had had shaken her determination not to be attracted to him.

But then he took two split logs from the pile he'd brought in earlier and something else caught her eye.

"Mouse!" she cried as it ran out of the stack.

Conor spun around, looking for it, one of the logs in his hand held like a weapon, poised to hit it.

"No, don't kill it!" Maicy said, running around the utility table. "It's just a baby."

A baby frantically looking for cover.

"It can't be a pet, Maicy," Conor countered reasonably.

"I'll open the door and you chase it in that direction."

"Chase it?" he said as if she were out of her mind, but at the same time trying to scare it in the direction of the cabin's front door as Maicy ran to open it.

"This is crazy. One swat and—"

"Catch it if you can, then," Maicy ordered.

"Do you know what kind of diseases mice carry? Maybe you should try to shoo it away," he added facetiously.

Maicy did try that and while it didn't have the same effect as it had had on the lion, stomping her feet sent the mouse in Conor's direction, where he swiped at it to send it to her. Back and forth they volleyed the small gray rodent until Maicy got it close enough to the door to scare it out of the cabin.

"Good! Good! Go find your mom!" she called after it, ahead of the sound of Conor laughing.

"Seriously? You *save* mice now? I seem to recall a time when you were afraid of them."

Maicy couldn't help her sheepish expression because she'd been caught in a long-ago lie.

She closed the cabin door, shivering. And avoided the topic by saying, "It's *still* snowing and it's so cold it's never going to stop."

"And you just let out all our heat to save a damn

mouse. Come by the fire," he advised, going over to stoke the flames and add that log she hadn't let him use as a weapon. "And tell me how it is that you lost your fear of mice."

Just when she'd thought he might have moved on from that...

"Yeah... Hmm... I was never afraid of them," she said, tiptoeing around the subject as she joined him.

She sat on the floor in front of the hearth, her legs curled to one side, bracing her weight on one hand to lean toward their only source of warmth.

Once the fire was roaring, Conor sat on the floor, too, near enough to share the heat, one leg curved in front of him, one bent at the knee to brace his elbow. "You played me?"

"I *let* you play rescuer," she amended.

All the Madison sons had been over six feet tall in high school and with the workouts their stepfather had put them through preparing them for the military they'd been better developed than most boys their age. It had been nothing for Conor to scoop her up into his arms to protect her from the dreaded mouse when she'd pretended to be scared that day in his barn.

Up in his arms where she'd been able to wrap her own arms around his neck. And thank him with a kiss. A lengthy kiss full of teenage fervor...

"And I don't recall any complaints then," she pointed out.

"You played me," he repeated, this time an accusation, not a question, holding his ground.

Maicy couldn't suppress a smile. It *was* funny that she'd put one over on him even though the new Maicy would never, ever act like a damsel in distress for any reason.

Conor was staring at her but suddenly there was something different than challenge and playful accusation in those blue eyes. Something that was softer and warmer than the heat of the fire. "God, I always loved to see you smile like that... I've missed it..." he said in a quiet voice.

He was making it so hard to keep hating him. To keep being mad at him.

The smile went away with those thoughts. With the realization that she didn't feel the animosity she'd felt at the start of this and for so many years before. Feeling unbalanced, she stared into the fire as if he hadn't said anything.

"And now it's gone and that's all I get?" he cajoled.

She glanced back at him, a part of her wanting to skewer him with a cutting remark just to keep her own controls in place.

But for some reason she didn't. For some reason, once she was looking into those remarkable blue eyes of his, seeing that lingering softness and warmth—and maybe something that might have been affection—in them, she couldn't even think of one.

Then he brought his free hand up and under her hair to the back of her neck and kissed her.

There was sweet familiarity and more in that kiss. So much more that he'd apparently learned over time because this was worlds better than any kiss they'd shared in the past. Worlds better than any she'd had since.

With lips that were parted just enough.

With a lazy sway that soothed and drew her in and tantalized her all at once.

With the perfect amount of confidence and command that invited her lips to part, too.

Because yes, she was kissing him back. And while her resolve not to get emotionally entangled hadn't changed, there was also nothing in her now that wanted to stop.

Which, in itself was alarming, so after a few more minutes, she did pull back.

"Yeah…that's not what we're gonna do," she muttered as if she hadn't just given as good as she'd gotten.

Conor's only response was a raise of his chin that left her unsure whether he was agreeing or conceding or maybe just humoring her. But it didn't matter because *she* wasn't going to let it happen again.

She stood up. "It's probably better if we say goodnight."

He nodded.

"Thanks for not killing the mouse when you could have," she said.

Conor chuckled. "Sure. I didn't have to anyway— we make a pretty good team. Still."

Maicy didn't comment on that, either. She merely said, "See you in the morning."

"See you in the morning," he parroted as she went into the bedroom and changed into her pajamas. Afterward, she peeked through the fireplace to see if Conor was still sitting where she'd left him.

He wasn't.

She repositioned to watch him arranging his pillow and blanket on the sofa.

It was only when he'd finished that, stood straight

and tall, and crossed his arms over his middle to take hold of the hem of his shirt to peel it off that she yanked up, refusing to let herself watch that.

But not because she was taking the higher moral ground.

After that kiss she knew that if she did too much peeping she might not be able to keep herself from going back out into that living room and kissing him again.

And that was just not what she was going to let herself do.

Regardless of how much a part of her might want to.

Chapter Six

"Die alone!"

Her own outcry woke Maicy with a jolt.

"Shh, hey, you're okay. You aren't dying. And you aren't alone."

She *had* been alone when she'd fallen asleep on the couch on Thursday afternoon, so Conor's voice startled her almost as much as her nightmare had. Even though his tone was soothing and comforting.

Embarrassed, Maicy sat up and put her feet on the floor before she said, "When did you get back?"

It took her eyes a minute to focus before she spotted him across the cabin. His multiple layers of clothes and outer gear were covered in snow.

"I just came in the door. I need the tote for tonight's stock of wood. Are you okay?"

"Fine," she answered. To prove it she got off the

couch, retrieved the canvas sling and took it to him. "I just dozed off and had a dream." A bad dream.

"Any more dizziness?"

Maicy made a face. Earlier that day, he'd caught her in a dizzy spell when she'd wobbled into a wall. Since she'd had him believing that the dizzy spells were gone and now he'd learned that she was still having them, he was back to insisting that she sit idly and rest.

"Honestly, it happens less and less. I just stood up too fast before. And I really do feel better every day. If I was home I'd have gone back to work yesterday and I'd be at full speed today."

"Not with me as your doctor you wouldn't," he claimed. "A head injury is nothing to fool with, Maicy. Now that I know you're still getting dizzy I better not see your butt off that couch for anything but bathroom breaks."

She rolled her eyes at him.

She hadn't followed that order when he'd given it earlier. Once he'd left again she'd done what she'd done the day before—spruced up.

After showering, dressing in jeans with a chunky snow-white cable-knit sweater on top and putting on makeup, she'd spent an hour doing a hairstyle she rarely had time for, elaborately twisting and weaving her hair in back while still leaving it loose enough for artful, wavy, come-hither wisps to fall around her face.

"And tonight," he went on, "I'm cooking and you're eating—no more of that picking at your food the way you've been doing this whole time. You need a substantial meal. We're having stew—meat, potatoes, vegetables—and you're eating every bit of what I put in front of you."

She was about to say *okay, Dad*, until the word "meat" registered.

"What kind of meat?" she asked suspiciously. "There's only canned ham and dried salami and pepperoni—stew needs real meat. And I'm not eating squirrel or something," she warned.

"It's not squirrel. It's just meat," he hedged, accepting the log tote from her.

"Deer? Elk?" she asked although neither of those seemed likely.

"No rifle, no arrows, so no, no deer or elk—although I did see a beauty today—"

He was trying to change the subject and she wasn't going to let that happen. "I'm not eating it unless I know what's in it," she said with a hint of challenge. But it was still an even-tempered challenge, not belligerent or hostile like she might have been days ago. While neither of them had mentioned that kiss the night before, it had changed the tenor between them. Maicy's antagonism was gone and she was feeling more convivial than she had been. More like years ago. Without the affection, of course.

Even if that kiss *had* been on her mind since the minute it had ended.

"When did you get so stubborn?" he challenged back, also amiably.

"I learned from the best—you," she said, and even that had a friendly tone. "What kind of stew are you forcing me to eat?"

"Rabbit."

"You killed a bunny?"

"It was a mean, vicious snaggletoothed beast that attacked me in the woods. A pure case of him or me—"

"Bull," she said.

"It'll taste like chicken and you're going to eat it. You need the protein. You just pick at the beans when we have them and the only time you've cleaned your plate since this started is last night when you ate cake. And I'm not letting you have the rest of that cake tonight unless you eat my stew. Now go sit down again. I'll be back in a few minutes."

Maicy gave him a flippant salute and stayed where she was. He shook his head at her as he turned and left through the mudroom.

Maicy was in the bedroom when he came in again twenty minutes later because she didn't want to see this particular meal before it was safely in a pan.

"You might want to stay in there a little while," he warned from the kitchen. "I'll let you know when the coast is clear."

"Gross," she called back.

"Pretend it came packaged from the grocery store. It'll be delicious."

Since she was close to the bathroom anyway, she went to the only mirror in the place—the one over the sink in there—to make sure her nap hadn't smudged her makeup or ruined her hair.

But looking at herself now she stopped a little short.

Maybe she'd done too much...

All she would need was a cocktail dress added to the hair and makeup, and she could have gone to a New Year's Eve party.

What had she been thinking, glamming up like this in the middle of nowhere?

Dumb question.

She'd been thinking about Conor. And about another evening alone here with him tonight. And how much she'd liked him taking notice last night.

And about that kiss.

And how much she'd been craving another ever since that one had ended...

Oh, Maicy...

Hoping Conor hadn't taken too close a look at her yet, she retrieved cotton balls from her suitcase and used them to mute some of the eye shadow, blush, bronzer and highlighter until she looked less party-ready. She left her hair, though, because there was enough whimsy to the style to pass for casual. Plus, he might not notice the makeup, but he was sure to realize if she changed her hair and he might even think she'd redone it *for* him. So the hair stayed.

Then she glared at her reflection in the mirror to reprimand herself for primping as if she were preparing for a date with a new man she really, really liked and wanted to really, really like her.

Only this man was Conor Madison. Not someone she really, really liked. Not someone she wanted to really, really like her. Those days were done and gone. But okay, yes, she admitted that it had been satisfying that he hadn't been able to resist her last night. That had been her goal and she'd met it. And returning to being resistible hadn't been her aim today, that was for sure. So maybe she'd gone a little extreme.

What was the point of trying so hard to wow him?

For most of that first year after they'd broken up she'd hoped and prayed and wished for him to change his mind about marrying her, to surprise her and come back, to tell her he didn't know what had gotten into him, that he'd been wrong, that he loved her above all else, couldn't live without her and would give up everything to have her.

But when that hadn't happened she'd toughened up. She'd stopped even the slightest fantasies about them getting together again. Certainly now a relationship with him, of all people, was inconceivable. So why did she want him drooling over the sight of her?

Then something else occurred to her.

Maybe she was looking at this the wrong way. Maybe it didn't have anything to do with Conor or the feelings she'd had for him as a girl.

Maybe this was about walking in on Gary kissing his old flame. Maybe this was about rebounding and finding a way to feel attractive and desirable again.

Now *that* made sense!

Sure, it could be argued that Gary kissing his ex meant that he hadn't gotten over Candace, not that he wasn't attracted to Maicy. But it was still a blow to her self-esteem. It had still left her with some doubts about herself, even if she *had* felt relieved that she hadn't had to go through with the wedding. She'd still been cheated on.

And when a person got cheated on, she rationalized, the first thing they needed was to feel appealing and attractive again.

That was where rebounds came in.

And maybe the universe had given her that in the form of Conor.

Conor, who owed it to her after devastating her himself.

Plus it could be accomplished so tidily when she was already stuck in the wilderness with him with nothing better to do than hair and makeup that made it impossible for him *not* to take notice. Then, by the time she got back to Denver it would be done—rebound wrapped up.

And she could move on.

It was all so efficient and convenient. She liked that.

Looking at it like that she decided that what she was doing was nothing but the logical and necessary step to getting over finding her fiancé kissing someone else on their wedding day. It was understandable. And she didn't have to worry about it. She could just roll with it and let it accomplish what it accomplished.

It wasn't the big deal she had been sort of worried that it might be. It didn't signal that she still had feelings for Conor. It was just an ego thing.

And the fact that he'd rejected her, too—even if not for someone else—was no doubt playing a role, she went on reasoning. It was only natural to want him to see her as someone he'd missed out on, to regret not doing everything he could have done to hang on to her. This was really the universe killing two birds with one stone—she could feel as if Conor was seeing what he'd missed, and she could transition from Gary.

"Just don't overdo it," she whispered to her reflection.

Did kissing Conor qualify as overdoing it? Probably.

But she'd already told him that that was not what they were going to do and she'd meant it. Kissing blurred the very clear line between them. Between then and now. Between control and no control.

And she was never comfortable not being in control.

Plus it was one thing to fill empty hours putting on makeup and doing her hair, another thing entirely to spend them kissing. Kissing could lead to occupying empty hours with more than kissing...

A shiver ran up her spine at just the thought of Conor holding her when he kissed her—something that hadn't happened last night.

At just the thought of Conor kissing her in a way that was more than simple and sweet—the way he'd kissed her last night.

At the thought of feeling his hands on her body and taking him to that downy bed with her where she could satisfy the curiosity about what it would be like to have him make love to her. The curiosity she'd been left with all these years because they hadn't gone that far as kids even though they'd both wanted to something fierce...

No, no, no, no, no! Stop that! she ordered herself, reining in the insane wanderings of her mind.

Whatever was going on was *not* going there! *They* were not going there. It was not even getting as far as a second kiss.

"Remember," she again whispered to her reflection.

Remember how he'd deserted her when she'd needed him eighteen years ago. And remember the realization that had occurred to her earlier, when he'd left on to-day's hunt for cell service.

She needed to remember how crystal clear he was

making it that when he truly cared about someone—
the way he did about his brother—he pulled out all the
stops for them. All the stops he hadn't been willing to
pull out for her when she'd needed him most.

There was no greater indication of how little he'd
felt about her years ago than that. If Conor had truly
loved her, nothing would have mattered but her—the
way the cold and the weather and the hardship of being
out in it every day just to find even a minute of phone
service to check on his brother didn't matter as much
as getting that check on Declan.

And no way was she letting herself be vulnerable
to someone who had already proved the limitations of
his feelings for her.

So thanks to the universe for providing a little balm
to her self-esteem.

But that was as far as anything with Conor was
going.

Having made herself feel better about the hours of
primping, she left the bathroom and went to sit on the
edge of the bed, calling to him from there.

"Did you get through to your brother today?"

"Not to him, he's still heavily sedated and in ICU.
But I talked to his doctor. The lab results came back—
the ones that cultured the bacteria to narrow down the
antibiotics that'll work best against it. That gave them
a better idea of how to treat him. He's not better but
he's not worse."

"That's a little bit of good news."

"Nothing to celebrate but, yeah, at least his condition is stable," Conor repeated as if he was hanging
on to that. "He's not out of the woods by any means,

though. I should still be there where I could watch him, stay by his bedside."

Which Maicy had no doubt he would be doing if he was in Maryland. Pulling out all the stops for someone he truly cared about…

"Did you talk to Rickie in Northbridge?" she asked then, thinking that the sooner people could dig out of the small town and get them out of this cabin, the happier she'd be.

"I couldn't even finish the call with Vince before service cut out. I was just glad I got as much information as I did."

"And it's still snowing…" Maicy lamented to herself more than to him. "We *are* going to get out of here before spring, aren't we?" she asked, feeling some fear that this storm would never end.

Conor chuckled. "We'll get out before spring," he said, not seeming concerned about that. "You know how it is around here—the storm will stop, the sun will shine and a week later it'll be like it never happened except that the ski slopes will be plush."

"And you'll be with Declan in Maryland and I'll be home in Denver," she added to remind herself that when this was over they would likely never see each other again.

For some reason she didn't understand that made her feel a little sad.

But she shoved it aside and said, "Smells like your stew is cooking."

"It is. A little more cleanup and the coast will be clear."

He went on to tell her that he'd had to go as far as the main road today before finding phone service so he'd checked on her car. Unfortunately, it was completely covered, and the road leading to the cabin was also impassable. Even when Rickie could get out to them, he'd probably only be able to pick them up and bring them into town. There'd be no traveling home for either of them anytime soon.

"It's another reason you need something nutritious to eat—we're probably going to have to snowshoe out to meet Rickie when he *can* get around the rockslide."

"What about our cars?"

"Yeah, that'll be another story. I'd say a day more to dig out yours so it can be towed into town, and the road up here will have to be plowed to get mine out."

"So we'll have to stay in Northbridge?" That was a horrible thought given that it was such a small town and Gary, Candace and dozens of almost-wedding guests were there.

Maicy's dread of it must have sounded in her voice because Conor said, "Sorry, but yeah, I'm sure we will. Were you staying with Gary or his family?"

"No, I was in the minister's guesthouse—where I lived that last year of high school."

"That's not too bad then, is it?"

The accommodations weren't the problem.

Maicy didn't respond and after a few minutes of silence Conor said, "Okay, done in here. Stew is cooking. I'm going to shower."

The arrival of that particular time of day didn't thrill Maicy. She couldn't keep her mind off thoughts of him naked during the shower and then he always came out clean-shaven and looking and smelling so good that it weakened her defenses.

But that was her problem to deal with. She could hardly tell him he couldn't shower. Or why.

So she steeled herself, stood up from the bed and went into the main room.

"I could make cornbread again to go with—"

"You can sit on the couch," he said firmly before she'd even finished the suggestion. "I already threw together a mix for focaccia and put it in the oven. I'll tell you what you can do, though—from the couch. You can try to decipher my handwriting and start a more legible list of what we've used. Then when we do get out of here I can give it to Rickie so he knows what to replenish."

"You've been keeping track?" It was something Maicy hadn't thought to do. But of course the man-with-the-plan had.

"I have been."

Now that she thought about it, though, she realized it was the right thing to do. "Sure. And then we'll split the cost to reimburse him."

Conor didn't comment on that as he slid a piece of scribblings-laden paper across the utility table to her. Then he opened the cupboard drawer and took out a tablet and a pencil.

"Now take it over to the couch and sit!" he ordered as he handed her the writing equipment.

Grateful for something to occupy her mind while he showered, she immediately tackled the task.

And it did help because his handwriting was so bad she had to put all of her attention on figuring out each item on the list.

But unfortunately she was finished when he returned and at a loss for a distraction. And there he was again, smelling clean and looking all the more rugged and sexy because he hadn't shaved tonight.

An anti-kissing measure of his own maybe?

He wasn't supposed to do *that*! He was supposed to be dying to kiss her again!

Instead he just looked all the sexier with that stubble and *she* was dying to have him kiss her even with that.

You're hopeless, Maicy...

Also not aiding the resistance, he was dressed in jeans and a plaid flannel shirt that didn't hide a single muscle and looked so soft she itched to touch it.

The shirt, not him or those muscles inside of it, she told herself, knowing she was lying as she watched him finish the cooking and dish up dinner.

She protested the amount of stew he'd ladled into her bowl as they took the stew and chunks of focaccia to the coffee table, while he continued his threat that she could only have dessert if she finished it all.

"I think you're forgetting that it's *my* wedding cake," she told him.

"Yeah, about that..." he said as they settled in to eat. "Are you still doing okay with all that or was feeling relieved just a passing stage?"

The relief hadn't been a stage. In fact, the further she got away from her wedding day, the clearer it became to her that marrying Gary had been a bad idea. That she really hadn't entered into it because she'd wanted to marry him, but to avoid hurting him the way Candace had, the way Conor had hurt her when he'd turned down her proposal.

The more soul-searching she'd done, the more she'd acknowledged that her feelings for Gary had been nothing more than comfortable affection. And while she had enjoyed his company, making a choice that had just felt practical wasn't really the smart way to go, regardless of what she'd thought before.

Although she was still worried about what it all said about her and wondered if Drake had been right...

But rather than say any of that, she said, "I'm still okay with not going through with the wedding. Actually as time goes by I can see where it was definitely good that it didn't happen."

"Okay," he said, seeming to take her at her word. "Then moving on to your health—if you really are feeling as good as you want me to think you are, why were you having a nightmare about dying alone here? People who are feeling better *stop* worrying about dying."

His interpretation of what she had been dreaming was all wrong but she wasn't sure she wanted to tell him what she really had been dreaming about.

But why should it matter? she thought. And talking—having something to talk about—was better than *not* talking. And kissing.

She'd dreamed that she was walking down the aisle in a soiled, torn, bloodied wedding dress, to a groom who had started out as Gary. And then become Drake. And then morphed into Conor before it was all three of them waiting for her at the altar shouting *Die alone!* as if they were a united front putting a curse on her.

She didn't want to get into the whole thing, so she said, "The dream wasn't about my health..."

She really didn't like talking about this. But if it kept them from kissing...

She took a breath and forged ahead.

"The only other serious relationship I've had was with a guy named Drake. When I broke up with him he showed some temper and said some pretty cruel things. One of them was that I was going to die alone—"

"And you dreamed he was saying that again?"

Him and Gary and you...

"Pretty much."

"So maybe you're *not* so all right with the wedding not happening?"

"It isn't that," she said as she ate some of the focaccia that tasted a little like the box that the mix had been packaged in.

"What is it, then?"

"I'm not sure how to put this... I'm okay not marrying Gary. But because I didn't get there, it's like...I guess it kind of gives more weight to what Drake said before him."

"Drake was just before Gary?"

"He was. I didn't get into any serious relationships until the last—" she did the math "—five years, I guess." And now that she thought about it, Gary had probably been the rebound from the split with Drake. Certainly she'd thought that the relationship with Gary proved Drake wrong and that had made her feel better about the ending with Drake.

Then she realized that Conor might be thinking it had taken her all the years before Drake to get over him and she didn't want that so she said, "Through both rounds of college I had to balance work along with school so there just wasn't time for much else. I dated here and there but nothing serious. When I finished my master's I knew I wanted my own business so those next five years were devoted to focusing on that—with the occasional blind date Rachel pushed me into."

"That's a pretty sparse personal life," he observed.

"I know. Rachel thought so, too, so she gave me a year of an internet dating service for a birthday present."

"You met this Drake on the internet?"

"A lot of people meet that way, you know," she defended because he made it sound as if there was something wrong with that.

"I'm sure," he said defensively himself. "I was just having enough to deal with thinking about you and Gary, now there's *Drake*." He said the name derisively and Maicy again liked that even after all this time the thought of her with another man tweaked a little jealousy in him.

"Drake," she repeated, rubbing it in just a bit. "Drake Astly—"

"I've heard that name. There's an Astly Surgical Equipment…"

"That would be the family business."

"Big money. And a dating service? Somehow that doesn't track. I mean, I get that you were too busy and neglected your personal life—I've done that myself—but wouldn't someone with that kind of bankroll have a lot of options when it came to a social life?"

"Yes and no. He was busy, too, with charities and foundations and fund-raising along with his job. But he was almost forty, his wife had actually decided she not only didn't want kids, she didn't want a husband, either. He'd been divorced for three years, all his friends were married, and he said there weren't as many single women around as he'd thought. Like me, he'd run through all the fix-ups friends and family could arrange for him. He was getting discouraged and on a lark, on one of the weekends when the site was offering a free trial to attract more members, he did some browsing—"

"And found you... Yeah, I could see that selling internet dating for him. And the two of you got serious?" Conor asked before he stood and headed for the kitchen for more focaccia.

Maicy declined his offer to bring her some, too, but on his way to the kitchen, while his back was to her, she spooned the stew she was too full to finish into his bowl.

"We were serious," she confirmed. "We were together a little over three years, we did the whole couples thing with Rachel and her husband, Jake—dinners, movies, regular game nights. We even went on two trips as a foursome. Then Drake wanted to get married."

"Don't tell me you ran away from that wedding, too?" Conor said as he came back and sat down again to resume eating.

"No, I didn't!" she said as if Conor was crazy to suggest it. "I just said no."

"You weren't thinking about how bad it was to be turned down that time?" Conor goaded slightly.

"It was a very different situation," she said, a little defensively. "Drake wasn't down on his luck, he wasn't trying to turn things around. And he was so... He had such a clear vision of what he wanted—and it wasn't at all what I wanted."

"What did he want that you didn't?"

"He sort of wanted me to sign over my life to him."

Conor paused with a spoonful of stew partway to his mouth to frown at her. "He wanted you to sign over your life to him? What was he, a conman?"

"No, nothing like that. It was just that he not only wanted us to get married, he wanted me to sell my business, be a stay-at-home wife and mother, a lady-who-lunched and who represented him and his family name in *important* circles."

"You don't like lunch?" Conor teased, taking that bite of stew.

"I usually eat it at my desk."

This time the look he gave her came from the corner of his eye. "I never thought career would be the most important thing to you."

Because *he'd* been the most important thing to her.

"Things change," she said. "I learned that what's important is to be able to take care of myself—"

"But you were okay taking care of Gary," he reminded. "With him not taking care of *himself*."

"I'm all right being relied on—"

"Just not relying on anyone yourself."

"I rely on Rachel. But I'm not *dependent* on her and I don't want to be dependent on anyone—which I would have ended up being if I'd given up everything just to be *Mrs*. Drake. He said it didn't matter that I wouldn't have my own income, he and his family had a boatload of money and I didn't need to work. That he didn't *want* a wife who worked. But that's just not for me. Being a stay-at-home wife and mother is great if that's your choice—it's what Rachel wanted so she closed her bakery when she found out she was pregnant. Jake supports them and she's all right with that so I'm all right for her—"

"But for you? You wouldn't be *all right* with it?"

"It's just not something I could do. My mom depended on my dad—why, I never understood, but she

did. And every time he took off she was left hanging—
we were left hanging. She'd have to rush out and get
any job she could while she begged for an extension
on our rent until she could come up with the money.
Then my dad would show up and she'd quit the job to
make a home for him—that's always what she said—"

"And the two of you would be left hanging all over
again when he took off the next time—I know, I was
there for some of that."

And then there was Conor letting her down when
she'd most counted on him—that had cemented her
resolve never to be in a position of helplessness again.

But she skirted around that and said, "So no, I
couldn't be comfortable doing what Drake wanted."

"And that made him mad?"

"He said I was *too* independent. *Too* self-sufficient.
That it made me closed off. That I have such a hard
shell no one can crack it. He said that what he wanted
was to take care of me, that it wasn't about him making
me weak or dependent. That I had a really screwed-up
view of things and if I didn't change it I was just asking to die alone…"

Conor was scowling into his bowl. "He had a lot to
say," he said, his voice deep with disapproval. "You
weren't asking him to change his whole life for you, so
why should he have expected you to change yours for
him? If he wanted you, he should have wanted whatever
life the two of you could work out together."

"Exactly."

Conor paused before saying cautiously, "But *are*
you *too* independent and self-sufficient and so closed
off that you don't let anyone in?"

"Rachel knows me inside and out—that's not being closed off."

Although Rachel *hadn't* jumped in to disagree with Drake's assessment that she was overly independent and self-sufficient. While she'd agreed that Drake had gone too far, and that he had no right to ask her to give up work she enjoyed to live a society life she didn't want, Rachel had actually said that maybe Drake had a point. She, too, had worried that Maicy might never have a husband and family if she didn't bend a little on some of that. It had made Drake's accusation haunt her all the more.

"But Rachel is a friend," Conor pointed out. "Knowing you inside and out as a friend is different from the kind of give-and-take that a marriage is. And if you're only closed off with men—"

"Gary never said I was closed off."

"But could you only do that with him because he needed you more than you needed him?"

She'd never thought of that. She'd just thought that she was proving Drake wrong by being with Gary...

"You know," Conor said then, "you've made sure you aren't in the position your mother was in by getting your education, by owning your own business. I understand why you wouldn't want to throw any of that away and why it would frustrate you if anyone wanted you to. But there should be some middle ground between a guy who wants you dependent on him, and one who's dependent on you. And it's not good if you can't relax unless you feel like the guy is the only one who has anything to lose..."

She *had* felt that way about Gary.

She didn't want to admit it, but it was the truth.

And she really didn't want to talk more about this.

But she had an out because just then she glanced at the window across the room over the sink.

"It isn't snowing!" she said, turning around on the sofa to look through the larger window behind them.

Conor did the same thing. "I knew it had to stop sometime but I was beginning to wonder when that time was going to come," he said.

"You should see if you have cell service," she suggested.

"It's two hours later in Maryland—"

"Still, you could get an update on Declan." And she could have a reprieve from talking about her messed-up love life.

She took both their empty bowls and plates to the sink while he turned on her phone because the battery on his had gone out.

"No, still nothing," he said a moment later.

Maicy had put the dinner things in the sink and was looking through the window there, suddenly feeling uncomfortably shut in.

"I'm going outside," she announced. "I want some fresh air."

She went to the bedroom for her coat, returning to find Conor donning his peacoat, too.

"Maybe I'll have better luck outside," he said, holding up her phone.

She buttoned her knee-length coat all the way up and they went out the back door, where they saw that the sky had cleared of clouds to leave a canopy of stars overhead and an almost full moon.

Conor didn't try for phone reception again, though.

Instead, as Maicy star-gazed, he Maicy-gazed, facing her from the side.

"So tell me one more thing," he said then, not letting her off the hook. "If Drake Astly had been okay with you keeping your business and working, would you have married him?"

Would she have married Drake?

She'd had feelings for him. But like with Gary, those feelings hadn't compared to what she'd had for Conor. And he'd been her first serious relationship after Conor so she'd made more comparisons and that alone likely would have stopped her.

By the time she'd gotten to Gary, she'd decided that her feelings for Conor had been teenage melodrama—the kind of puppy love that feels all-consuming at the time, and isn't intended to last. If she never felt that way about a man again, it just meant she'd finally grown up. She needed to accept that and settle for the way things were now.

"You wouldn't have." Conor answered his own question when she didn't.

"No," she said quietly and for some reason she had the sense that he knew why. She went from looking up at the stars to looking at him to see if she was right. She thought she was because there was a small smile on his handsome face as he studied her.

"I *want* the blame for that if it's because the first time you really got involved with someone after you and me it came up short for you."

"You *want* blame?" she challenged.

"For that I do," he said as he stepped in front of her, blocking her view of the sky and leaving her with the view of his striking features in the moonlight.

"For just one minute don't play your cards too close to the vest and tell me I'm right," he encouraged.

"Maybe," was as much as she would give.

He laughed, drawing her eyes to his mouth, the supple lips that had felt so fabulous last night...

"Good enough," he proclaimed in a voice that had a lower, more intimate timbre.

He went on staring at her with another, more thoughtful smile.

"The first time I ever kissed you was a night like this—outside..."

"Only it wasn't frigidly cold and we were watching fireworks—or at least I was," she filled in.

"I couldn't believe how beautiful you were—more than any fireworks. You were the most beautiful girl I'd ever seen." He ran the backs of his fingers along her cheek. "Still are..." he whispered.

If he'd left the stubble tonight to help him keep from kissing her, it didn't work. Because that was just what he did then—leaning in to capture her mouth with his as he wrapped his arms around her and brought the full length of her body to him.

Unlike the sweet, simple kiss of the previous night this one had heat to it right from the start. And it only got hotter.

Hot enough for the need of his hand cradling her head when that kiss bent her backward.

Hot enough for parted lips to part even more and urge hers to part, too.

Hot enough to send his tongue to entice hers into a sexy joust.

Her hands came out of their coat pockets and found their way under his arms to his back. It felt like an expansive, solid wall that she hung on to as she kissed him as fervently as he was kissing her.

But there wasn't supposed to be any kissing at all, she reminded herself somewhere in the process of opening her mouth even wider, feeling the roughness of his stubble against her face.

No kissing and certainly none of the massage that that big hand of his was doing on her back. None of the headiness that came from her breasts pressed against his chest. None of her melting into him and discovering that the fit was still so perfect…

None of any of it! she silently shouted at herself, torn between what she knew had to be done and what she wanted—which was to go on and on and on kissing him like that and then move on to even more…

It had to be stopped…

In just another minute…

No, now! she argued with herself.

Winning—or maybe losing—that argument, she retrieved her arms from around him, laid her palms to his chest, and pushed her way out of that kiss.

"You didn't see if you could get a signal out here," she reminded, her voice breathy.

"Yeah," was all he said, a little breathless himself and sounding as if stopping was killing him.

Before she could weaken enough to lean into him again, Maicy said, "You should try," and turned toward the cabin's back door.

"You know," he said as she opened it, stalling her rather than turning on the cell phone to follow her instructions, "I think you're taking what that Drake guy said too personally."

Maicy laughed humorlessly. "Everything he said was about me—that's personal."

"Yeah," Conor agreed. "But as much as I hate to cut him any slack for anything, I think I have to."

Then, in a voice that was even deeper, even more quiet, he seemed to confess.

"Take it from somebody who knows—it isn't easy to lose you."

Chapter Seven

Northbridge Hospital.

When Conor woke up in the cabin on Friday morning, the last thing he'd expected was to be sitting in the emergency room's waiting area by sundown.

But there he was. The end of an eventful thirteen hours.

After five straight days of blizzard, Friday had dawned with a clear sky and sunshine that hadn't helped the frigid temperature. But as usual the first thing Conor had done was leave the cabin in search of cell service.

He *had* managed to find that slightly closer than usual, though, only to learn that Declan's condition was the same.

Then he'd called Rickie.

His old friend had had better news for him—the

rockslide blocking the road into and out of town had been cleared.

"I'm right here with my truck," Rickie had told him. "I don't know what the road's like—technically it's still closed between here and Billings. But the snowplow is headed out to start clearing from this end. If I follow behind I might be able to make it far enough to get to you."

Since his friend was willing to try, Conor had agreed to search for cell service every two hours to check in with him for a progress report. Then Conor had returned to the cabin to tell Maicy they might be getting out today.

That had set them both into motion, packing and cleaning and doing what was necessary to shut the rustic shelter down, with Conor hiking out as scheduled to check in with Rickie.

At nearly four that afternoon, Rickie had made it to the foot of the road leading to the cabin.

With that news, Conor had returned to the cabin to outfit Maicy with snowshoes. He'd done a final check to be sure the place was left the way they'd found it—minus the supplies they'd tallied on their list—and then the two of them headed out, with Conor toting his duffel and Maicy's suitcase—minus the ruined wedding dress that was too bulky to pack and so had been left behind.

But when they'd reached the highway and Rickie's truck, Rickie wasn't with it. Instead he called to them from the pile of snow that was covering Maicy's car like a huge dome.

While he'd been waiting for them to get to him,

Rickie had started to dig out Maicy's car. In the course of that he'd lost his footing, fallen and broken his leg.

And once more Conor had been grateful for his field training.

While Maicy had searched the truck for anything he could use for makeshift medical supplies, Conor had stabilized the leg and splinted it with the two planks of wood and bungee cords she found for him.

Then Maicy had come up with the idea of using a ramp she'd found in the truck bed as a stretcher and a plastic tarp as a sheet. Between the two of them they'd cocooned Rickie with the tarp and gotten him onto the ramp so Conor could drag him to the truck and then hoist his pain-ridden old friend inside.

It had been a rough go, but finally Conor had been able to drive the truck into town, delivering Rickie *and* Maicy to the emergency portion of Northbridge's small hospital, where he'd filled in the ER doctor about both cases and—over Maicy's protests—recommended that she have an MRI.

And now here he was once again in the position that he'd come to hate—only hoping that the people he'd handed over to other medical professionals would be cared for the way he thought they should.

Particularly Maicy.

Treating a broken leg like Rickie's followed standard procedures. But with a five-day-old head injury the amount of testing was up to the doctor who took over. To be thorough, an MRI should be done. Whether it would be or not was out of Conor's hands.

It was just so damn aggravating. And since he wasn't Maicy's family, he wasn't allowed in the treatment room to argue for what he believed was in Maicy's best interests. He was as removed from her medical decisions as he was from those of the military men and women he treated before sending them off for their extended care.

As he sat there it occurred to him that the way he felt over having his cases passed on to other hands wasn't the only thing eating at him at that moment, though. Now that the chaos of the day was done and they'd made it into town, he was finding himself also hating that he and Maicy *weren't* at the cabin anymore—as crazy as that seemed.

Sure it was a good thing that they were out of there. No fresh food, limited supplies, no power, no central heat. Primitive plumbing. Cut off from the world unless he'd really worked for a connection—even an unreliable one. Mountain lions, mice and the constant effort to clear away snow so they weren't buried up there—yeah, there was no question that it was good to leave that behind.

But as he sat there it was just setting in that they'd left something else behind, too.

Being alone together like that might have been the only thing that would let them start working through their past. Working through their past and, in the process, maybe reconnecting, too.

Not that they should be. He knew that. Not that he wanted them to be.

But now that it was over it struck him that there had been something nice about being stranded with Maicy.

And now what? he asked himself.

Now Northbridge, where he'd be alone at his family's farmhouse. Where she'd be back at the minister's guesthouse—since the minister and his wife had already shown up at the hospital to invite her to stay.

Now Northbridge, where things had fallen apart for them before.

Now Northbridge, where there were plenty of people to intrude. Not the least of which was the man she'd been about to marry. The man who could have realized his mistake by now and re-ended things with his ex. The man who could be champing at the bit to reunite with Maicy.

Over my dead body, Stern, you jackass...

Not that he actually thought Maicy would take Gary Stern back. Surely the relief she'd felt at not marrying him would keep her from making the same mistake twice. And the guy had given her a prime excuse not to regardless of what a sad sack he was.

But yeah, as crazy as it seemed, he was suddenly missing the cabin. Wishing they were back there, that he was showering the way he'd done at this time of day, coming out to an evening of just the two of them...

You can't have her, you know. That ship has sailed, he told himself.

Her anger at him seemed to have mellowed at the cabin but he still didn't think she'd forgiven him. He didn't think she'd accepted the whys and what-fors of him turning down her proposal. He'd noticed every gibe she'd fought not to say. He'd seen the look in those gorgeous green eyes when she'd talked about both of her other relationships, the look that said he'd done damage of his own.

And both times he'd kissed her she'd stopped him.

Of course it had to be her who stopped because he sure as hell wouldn't—couldn't—have. Eighteen years ago or eighteen hours ago, he'd never wanted anyone as much as he wanted her. He was trying not to acknowledge that but it was true.

Was it chemistry? Pheromones? Maybe it was forbidden fruit or unfinished business.

She'd been forbidden fruit when they were teenagers. Maicy's mother had been determined to protect her daughter from an unplanned pregnancy and had watched Maicy like a hawk. Her mother had threatened her unmercifully with what she would do if Maicy got pregnant. Maicy had had so much fear of it that she'd been determined to maintain her virginity until they were married.

He'd already lost his virginity just before they'd started dating but he'd been willing to wait for her—difficult as that was when he'd wanted her in the worst way. But he'd known she was worth it. He'd loved her so much that nothing was more than he could take to have her. Plus he'd been certain that they *would* get married, that the day *would* come when he'd get to make love to her, and that had sustained him. For the most part.

But that day hadn't ever come.

Instead things between them had ended in what had seemed like the blink of an eye. Turning the forbidden fruit into unfinished business.

And leaving him wondering for the last eighteen years.

So no, he likely wouldn't have stopped kissing her last night if she hadn't ended it. Unfinished business coupled with how much he still liked kissing her had put willpower at a minimum.

Now here they were in town and...

And he didn't know what.

He only knew that when the minister and his wife had shown up here to offer their guesthouse and wait to take Maicy home with them, he'd nixed the idea of them sticking around, assuring them he would bring her to their guesthouse when she was finished. He wasn't ready to just walk away.

Sure the day was coming—projections were to have the highway to Billings and the airport there open by Sunday. But for now?

There was still tonight. And tomorrow and tomorrow night.

And he knew this town, he knew how gossip traveled, so he knew that by now every person in it had heard about her running away from her wedding. No matter what happened from here on between her and Gary, it wasn't going to be a day at the beach for her to face the looks and whispers. Or maybe worse than that, depending on how the Stern family and friends viewed what had happened. Had Gary and Candace even admitted what they'd done, or had they shifted the blame on Maicy who wasn't there to defend herself? He didn't know, and neither did Maicy.

So for now, if Maicy would let him keep her company, let him be her support system, he wanted to do that. He wanted to be there for her the way he'd wanted to be there for her when her mom died.

And if it provided an excuse to have a couple more days with her?

He couldn't deny that he wanted that, too.

But hopefully being back in town—in separate houses, and with the eyes of the town on them—would help keep things more on track than they had been with the last two nights of kissing. Hopefully being back where their world had exploded would help him remember that it *had* exploded, and there was no turning back the clock.

No, not just *hopefully*. He needed to remember that. To keep in mind that they each had their own lives now and when they inevitably returned to them this whole week would fade into history with everything else.

He had to get back to Declan and make sure his brother was on his feet again. He had to deal with Kinsey and this business with the Camdens. He had to figure out what he was going to do about his own career. And Maicy had her business and her friend Rachel whom she talked so much about and the rest of the life she'd built for herself.

They were just not destined to be together the way they'd thought as wide-eyed kids.

But he could still have the next couple of days, and he still wanted to be the support system he should have been years ago.

And maybe when this was all over with, when she got back to the life she'd built for herself, she might feel as if, in some small way, he'd made up for a little of what had happened long ago.

But kissing wasn't a part of that and he knew he had to not do it again. He knew he had to make sure that he didn't start something that could get out of hand.

Because he sure as hell didn't want to give her something else not to forgive him for.

"Every time I talk about releasing you, your blood pressure goes up," the doctor observed, looking at the monitor Maicy was hooked to. "What about that makes you anxious?"

"It's a long story," Maicy answered, her tone indicating that she wasn't going to tell it.

But Rebecca, the emergency room doctor, pursued it anyway. "Does it have something to do with the man waiting for you?"

"The minister?" Maicy asked. The minister and his wife had arrived just before she'd been called into the exam room. They'd come to assure her that their guesthouse was hers for as long as she was in town, and said they'd wait for her to be finished here to take her home.

"No, the man who brought you in—he's a doctor? He wanted you to have an MRI," Rebecca prompted.

"Conor is waiting for me?" Maicy had assumed that Conor would have bowed out.

"I overheard him tell the minister and his wife that they didn't need to wait, that he wanted to be here when you came out, to make sure you're all right before driving you to their house." There was suspicion in the doctor's voice until she said, "And now the blood pressure's going down, so maybe it isn't him who's upsetting you?"

Maicy didn't want to tell the doctor how happy she was to hear that Conor had stayed. "No, it isn't him," she said simply, again offering no explanation.

"I'm new to town. It seems like a decent place, with a lot of decent people. Am I missing something? Is it the thought of being set loose here that's bothering you?"

"No." But because the MD seemed not to want to drop the subject and Maicy wanted out of there, she said, "There's just someone I left behind here that I'm not thrilled with having to see again."

"And you aren't likely to be able to avoid that some-one since it's a small town," the doctor concluded for her. "Sorry but I can't admit you just so you can hide out."

Maicy assured her that she understood so the doctor unhooked her from the monitor, produced her release papers to sign and then left her to get dressed.

She put on the jeans and an emerald green turtleneck sweater that she'd picked today knowing it accentuated her eyes. As the day had played out, the choice of the eye-accentuating sweater—and the carefully applied makeup—had just seemed silly and irrelevant.

But if Conor was still waiting for her...

No, being appealing to him wasn't important in the grand scheme of things. It might have been something to do to while away the time in the cabin, but now they were back in the real world. The one in which she'd run away from her wedding.

Having to deal with the aftermath of that was what was making her wish a little that she and Conor were back in the cabin. It wasn't that she was actually miss-ing the place. Or being alone there with Conor. But she *was* having pangs about not being there anymore. And those pangs were helped by the knowledge that Conor was out in the waiting room.

Because yes, the whole time she'd been in this exam room there was a part of her that had been feeling very down at the thought that there wasn't any reason for him to be waiting for her now. Without being stranded in the woods, she'd feared that he would have gone his way, she would be left to go hers and it would be business as usual for them both.

And business as usual did not mean being a part of each other's lives.

But he waited...she thought as she went to the small mirror on one wall of the exam room to check her hair.

It was a mess so she took a brush from her purse, straightening it out while telling herself that being soothed by learning that Conor was out in the waiting room wasn't about him. She was just glad she didn't have to walk out of here and face Northbridge alone.

She'd been grateful to have him by her side when the minister and his wife had shown up. It had helped her wade through that first embarrassment as they'd told her with some veiled disapproval that she wasn't the first bride to panic.

And once she left the hospital? She had no idea what might be in store for her.

Gary was much more cemented in the community than she was. He still had friends he kept up with. Plus his family, and family friends. None of whom likely knew that she'd found him kissing his former girlfriend. Most probably, everyone was going to blame her for leaving him at the altar. And even as fiercely independent as she was, it helped to think of maybe having one person in her corner. Even if it was only for the moment.

Though she'd known from the start that their time together was limited, it hadn't felt that way in the cabin. Up there, there was no question that they would have dinner together. That they would spend hours talking. That even good-night didn't mean more than going into another room—knowing when she did that he'd be there when she woke up the next morning.

Now there were no certainties.

Not that she wanted there to be, she told herself.

It was just that...

She closed her eyes, took a deep breath and exhaled before opening them again to her own reflection, forcing herself to be honest.

It was just that it had been kind of nice being with him.

It was weird. She hadn't forgotten what he'd done, but the time in the cabin had reminded her of all the good before that. She did have to concede—only to herself—that she'd ended up enjoying his company in the cabin. And she wasn't altogether happy that it was over. Separate from the fact that she was definitely not happy to be in Northbridge again or to contend with whatever might be coming her way.

"But it is what it is," she told her reflection firmly.

For now, she was glad he'd waited. But only for now. Then she'd be on her own again and she could handle it. She'd handled everything she'd had to handle since her mom had died and she could handle whatever she had to from here on, too.

She hooked her hair behind her ears with a businesslike determination, gathered her things and left the exam room.

It would all be fine, she told herself on the way out.

And the very real pulse-quickening she felt the minute she went into the waiting room and set eyes on Conor in his jeans and another of those muscle-hugging T-shirts of his? The very real feeling that one glance from him made her stronger and better able to face anything and everything?

It didn't mean a thing.

"You stuck around..." she said, crossing to him.

"Sure," he answered as if there was no question. "No MRI though, huh?"

"The ER doctor thought it was too late to bother."

"That's why an MRI should be done—a CAT scan will show new injury, an MRI will show older ones," he explained, clearly displeased.

"But I'm doing okay," Maicy said. "I haven't had a dizzy spell since that one yesterday. She seemed to check me out pretty thoroughly otherwise, so—"

"Yeah, just not what I would have done," he grumbled.

Maicy knew his annoyance was linked to his growing frustrations with his own job. But she wasn't alarmed by the care she'd received. So all she said was, "I just want out of here. I hate hospitals."

Conor nodded. "I still have Rickie's truck—his wife, Jane, came to get him. She'll take him home. He said I should use his truck to get you to the minister's place and me to the farm tonight. Tomorrow Rickie's brothers will come for the truck and me—we're all three going back to the cabin with a plow and a tow truck to see if we can get our cars into town."

Oh yeah, she was definitely having cabin-loss-fever because another twinge hit her at just the mention of the place.

But she was never going to be there with him again. Ever. And she reminded herself once more that the sooner she had her car and could put this entire thing behind her, the better.

"But for tonight," Conor was saying, "let's get something to eat that doesn't come out of a can or a dry mix."

"Sounds good," she admitted, thinking that more than the food, what sounded good to her was that he didn't intend to just drive her to the minister's guesthouse and drop her off. At least they were going to have dinner together one more time.

Sadly, nothing was open but fast food, so dinner ended up being burgers and fries ordered at the drive-thru that they took with them to the guesthouse.

The guesthouse was a one-bedroom cottage not much larger than the cabin, positioned with access from a side street that allowed Maicy and Conor to get to it without disturbing the minister's family. And since the minister had left the key with Conor to give to her, they went directly there.

"I've never been inside this place," Conor said as they went in. By the time Maicy had moved in, when the month's rent had run out on the apartment she shared with her mother, Conor had left for college.

"It's kind of cozy," Maicy said truthfully. "I wasn't allowed to have boys here before, though, so don't be surprised if they come and make you leave," she joked as she turned on lights and raised the temperature on the thermostat.

"What was it like that year you lived here?" he asked somewhat tentatively as they took off their coats. "Were you part of the minister's family? Did you have meals with them and just come here to sleep or—"

"I was *not* part of the family," Maicy said. "I was the babysitter, really, even though they called me the nanny and paid me by the month instead of by the hour. My job was to get the kids up, fed, dressed and to school in the mornings before I went to school myself, then pick them up after school and bring them home or to whatever after-school things were going on. If either the minister or his wife were home in the evenings, they took over. If they both had somewhere to be, I handled evenings. But that was it—it was only about the kids and filling in when their parents couldn't be here. Their *family time* was their family time and that didn't include me."

"You didn't have meals with them? Holidays?"

"I ate with the kids if I was sitting with them, but otherwise, no. They invited me for Thanksgiving, Christmas dinner, their Easter meal—me and anyone else in the congregation who didn't have a family so I had the choice between here and friends who invited me. But on a regular basis? They're nice people but they're pretty stuffy and formal, and no, I wasn't part of the family—there was no question about that."

"I'm sorry, Maicy. I pictured them treating you like their own."

"It was okay. I wasn't really looking to be part of anyone's family. Not after losing my mom." *And you.* "I liked having my own space," she said honestly. Then, with nothing more to say about it, she nodded toward the café-sized kitchen table, where two chairs waited. "Unlike the cabin, we have a table to eat at here."

"Yeah…" Conor said unenthusiastically. "But I'm kind of missing that place—"

"It's funny, isn't it?" Maicy said by way of admitting it herself.

"You, too?"

"A little."

"Then how about we eat at the coffee table for the heck of it?"

Maicy agreed, only rather than sitting side by side on the sofa the way they had at the cabin, they found themselves on the floor, on opposite sides of the coffee table.

"Be straight with me," Conor commanded as they settled in to eating. "*Are* you really feeling okay even after all we did today?"

"I really am," she said, omitting that she was slightly more worn out than she would have ordinarily been after the exertions of the day. She didn't want him to think she was tired, that he needed to leave. She was very aware that she wasn't in any hurry for that to happen.

"No headaches, no dizziness, no blurred vision, no flashes in my eyes, no memory problems, no nothing," she added. "Exactly what I told the doctor at the hospital. What I was telling her while you were apparently out in the waiting room chatting it up with *Jane*..." She said the other woman's name with heavy insinuation.

He laughed. "I was talking to Jane about Rickie. Whom she's married to."

"I was surprised to hear that. She wasn't interested in him when we were in high school. She was only interested in you..."

"And I was only interested in you," he countered.

Maicy tried to ignore the little wave of warmth that gave her. "It didn't discourage her. I heard that after we broke up—before you left for college—she put the pursuit into high gear."

"Is that what you heard?" he said rather than confirming or denying anything.

Which made Maicy suspicious. "She did, didn't she?"

"It didn't make any difference. She couldn't fill your shoes."

Maicy had heard about him rejecting the other girl, but she'd always wondered if it was true. "So who *did* fill my shoes?" she asked.

He smiled a secret kind of smile before he said, "I plunged myself into school and ROTC training—that kept me as busy as I knew it would," he said, not answering her question.

"For how long? A month before you—"

He laughed. "Longer than that. A lot longer than that."

"To this day you've been pining for me?" she challenged.

"Just a few days ago, you jumped to the conclusion that I have a pregnant wife and now I've just been pining for you?" he said.

"You did say last night that you understood my neglecting my personal life because you had, too," she reminded.

"I may have neglected it, but I've had one."

"That you're being cagey about," she accused.

"I'm not being cagey about it," he said defensively.

"Yes you are. You've heard about my relationships, I want to hear about yours," she claimed, not completely sure that was true. But she thought that it might help her fight his appeal if she had a clearer image of him as a single man involved with other women. A single man who wasn't hers...

"Who filled my shoes for the first time?" she demanded.

Conor made a face. "Really? You want to talk about this?"

"I told you about Drake and Gary."

"You nearly married those two."

"And nothing else counts? Besides, you always wanted a family. Do you expect me to believe you've never come close to getting married?"

Rather than answer that he rewound and answered her earlier question. "I didn't date anyone until my junior year of college—like I said, I devoted myself to school and training."

"And in your junior year…" Maicy persisted.

"There was Michelle. She was on the same fast track to becoming a doctor so we had almost all of our classes together. Eventually she became a…you know, friend-with-benefits. More because it was convenient for us both."

"Convenient…" Maicy repeated. "She was okay with that?"

"It was her suggestion."

"Ah, another Jane in hot pursuit. Only you let *Michelle* catch you."

"There was no pursuit. Just convenient stress release," he said with a laugh.

"Very romantic," Maicy said facetiously. "And after Michelle?"

"There've been a few others," he answered ambiguously. "Another resident when I was doing my residency. A nurse here and there. A lab tech and a social worker—"

"It was the lab tech and the social worker that you got close to marrying," Maicy guessed.

He laughed. "Not close, but... How did you know that?"

She'd heard a slightly more somber note in his voice when he'd mentioned them. But she merely shrugged and smiled coyly to let him know she wasn't giving away her secrets.

"Yes, it was the lab tech and the social worker— they both wanted to get married," Conor confirmed.

"Don't tell me—they proposed to you, too, and you turned them down the same way you turned me down."

"There were no *proposals*," he amended. "There were just ongoing conversations—marriage and kids were what they saw for the future—"

"But you didn't see it for yours?"

"Yeah, I said it was what I saw for my future, too," he said but in a way that hedged. "It just...didn't work out with either of them."

"Why not?"

"With Glenda—the lab tech—we'd only been going out six months when she wanted a firm timeline of when we'd end up at the altar."

"And you weren't ready to guarantee that the relationship would get there."

"I liked her but it had only been six months. And I *only* liked her—I mean, maybe it could have turned into more, but... When I wouldn't give her a firm timeline, a definitely-we'll-get-married, she opted to move on." He didn't say that as if he had any regrets.

"And the other one, the social worker?" Maicy prompted.

"Social-worker-who-became-a-navy-lieutenant. Janice was a social worker here before she joined the navy and was sent overseas as an aide to an admiral.

She came with him on a field visit in Afghanistan. An Afghan national—not much more than a kid— approached the admiral with an IED strapped to his waist. The IED malfunctioned and only killed the kid and injured the admiral."

"And you treated the admiral."

"I did—that was how Janice and I met. He was too badly injured for ground transport and we couldn't get a helicopter in right away, so I treated him. With Janice there the whole time—"

"That is not a meet-cute story," Maicy said.

"It *is* how we met, though. And actually, because we sort of hit it off despite the circumstances and kept in contact even after she and the admiral were evaced, that was the first time I heard about what a patient of mine went on to and got irritated by it."

"When was this?"

"A little over three years ago. The admiral made it but his care didn't follow the course I would have set for him and I think he had a rockier road than he should have had—he ended up losing the arm I'd saved and with different, more cautious care, I don't believe that would have been the case."

"So your job frustrations have been building for that long?"

"They have. After that I started checking up—where and when I could—on what happened to my patients after they left me. And yeah, some of the things I've learned have made me more and more aggravated. But it hasn't mattered up until now because my years of obligation to the navy weren't up—I didn't have a choice except to go on doing what I signed on to do."

"But now you could make a change," Maicy finished

for him. She also realized that he'd effectively steered the subject away from his romances and she wasn't going to let him, so as she picked up the wrappers left from their finished dinner to throw away, she said, "If the social-worker-turned-aide had to stick with the admiral wherever he was, how did the two of you go on to have a relationship?"

Conor laughed. "And here I thought I was getting away from that." He sighed but continued as she rejoined him with a box of chocolate mints she'd left in the cabin from her pre-wedding days here.

"We just kept in contact," Conor said, taking a mint to eat while Maicy did the same before rejoining him on the floor. "We got together whenever we could. The admiral refused to be sent stateside so that kept Janice not too far away. She had leave time. I had leave time—"

"You must have really liked each other," Maicy said. The same way she'd been able to tell by his voice which women in his life he'd considered marriage with, she could tell that he'd cared about this Janice, and it raised some uninvited jealousy in her.

"I told you, we hit it off," he confessed in a way that confirmed for her that the relationship had been serious. Bothering her all the more.

"And it went on how long?" she asked.

"About two years. Which was why Janice thought it was time to take the next step."

"The next step being to get married."

He nodded but didn't offer more than that.

"So why didn't you?" Maicy asked with some caution.

Another shrug but no answer for a while before he

said flatly, "I just didn't see it and we parted ways." His tone made it clear that he didn't want to say more than that. Then, in a cheerier voice, he said, "And there you have it—nothing as exciting as an AWOL bride."

Maicy mock-flinched. "An AWOL bride?"

"That's what you are, isn't it? Absent without leave?"

"I think I had leave," she countered.

Conor grinned at her. "I think you did, too. I'm just giving you a hard time," he said, looking at her differently than he had been a moment before, his blue eyes softer, warmer, but so intent that he seemed to be committing every feature to memory.

"And you don't have any room to talk," Maicy teased in return. "At least I got close to getting married. But you? Someone who doesn't know you might say *you* have commitment issues."

"But you *do* know me," he said in a deeper, more intimate voice.

"I know how committed I've seen you be with Declan and your family. I know it's commitment to your other patients that's causing you to question what kind of medicine you want to practice, and your commitment to the military that's making it harder for you to consider a change. But with women..." she finished with a goading inflection.

"With women," he went on, still in that quiet, confidential way, "the commitment issue is that once upon a time I made a commitment to some red-haired girl. And even though she called it quits on me, I've never been sure that broke it from my side." He slid out from behind the coffee table and leaned forward, saying as he moved nearer, "Plus the honest-to-God truth about why I never got married is that *no one* has been able to fill that red-haired girl's shoes and replace her..."

No, hearing about him with other women hadn't helped fight his appeal. It hadn't given Maicy a clearer image of him as not hers. Not when he said that. And as irrational and ill-advised and unwise as she knew it was, she just wanted to reclaim him.

So when he raised that left arm from his knee to run the backs of his fingers along her cheek and came closer still, she didn't fight the urge to lean forward, to meet him halfway and kiss him.

And not only did she not fight that urge, she set aside every argument, every warning she'd been fostering, and just let herself be drawn into kissing this man.

Kissing him even more heatedly than they'd kissed under the stars the night before. Even more passionately as lips parted and tongues met again to mingle madly.

His arms wrapped around her and pulled her with him to lounge back against the front of the sofa, holding her close.

Her own arms slipped under his so she could lay her hands on shoulders so much broader than they had been when they were teenagers.

Only unlike kissing him then, Maicy didn't have to be on the alert or worry that they might get caught. She could merely lose herself in that kissing, in that tongue-play, in the feel of all those muscles and sinews that he'd developed, in the feel of the man he'd become.

And in the feel of his hands on her...

On her back where his fingers did a massage that was taking away every last bit of tension, turning her into soft, fluffy, pliable marshmallow.

Then one hand moved to her side, to the outermost

curve of a breast that had come to know his immature touch only in scattered, stolen moments. Breasts that both now cried out to know more of his touch than that.

Her nipples turned into insistent little pebbles and pressed through the lace of a honeymoon bra, through her sweater and into his chest. He must have felt the evidence of her arousal, if the increasing ravenousness of that kiss, if the even wider opening of his mouth, if the even more aggressive plundering of his tongue, was any indication.

There was no timidity in the grown Conor's hand as he brought it to cup her breast then, to enclose it in a grip that was tender and strong at once. A grip that she pressed into, wanting so much to feel flesh against flesh that she nearly tore herself away from that fevered kiss to tell him.

But Conor was in tune with her and she didn't have to say a word because after only a moment his hand slipped underneath her sweater.

He took a little time to test the lace of her bra, to run a fingertip over the edge of the cup, before he lowered it and gave her what she was looking for—the free and unfettered feel of his big, warm hand cupping her flesh.

Oh, yeah, he'd learned a few tricks...

Kneading and caressing, he teased and soothed her breast by turns. He tantalized and titillated. He pinched and rolled and tugged her nipple then cradled it in the tenderness of his palm.

And with each moment that passed came needs in Maicy that were both new and old, all of them more demanding than ever before, and it almost shocked her to discover how much she wanted him to make love to her.

Too much, maybe.

She knew she'd probably regret this later—especially having it happen in the minister's guesthouse, a place that seemed too sacrosanct to do what her body was crying out to do.

So this time she did end that scorching kiss to whisper, "We can't do this…here…"

She should have just said *no* rather than pretending the location was the obstacle. But she couldn't bring herself to refuse him outright. Not when she wanted him so much.

"Come out to the farm with me, then," he said in a voice ragged with desire.

Maicy shook her head. "No," she said more definitively. "There's already enough to answer for…"

"I don't give a damn!" he said, sounding desperate to have her.

Maicy laughed a little wryly, understanding. Still she said, "I do. And this is the—"

"Yeah, I know," Conor complained, "this is part of the church."

"And I'm the guest of the minister," she added with a sinner's laugh. "We have to behave."

Conor groaned. "I'm *really* missing the cabin now," he muttered.

But he gave her breast one last squeeze, readjusted her bra with expertise he hadn't had as a teenager before taking his hand out from under her sweater.

That triggered a moan of regret from Maicy that escaped on its own and prompted Conor to recapture both her mouth and her breast on top of her clothes again.

With some things slightly more in control, Maicy indulged and for a while they went on kissing and caressing as they had as teenagers.

Until her control began to waffle and she knew she had to hold her ground.

So once more she stopped things.

"You have to go," she told him.

He took a deep breath, closed his eyes, let his head fall back and said a "Yeah, okay…" that was full of complaint.

Then he sighed, let go of her and sat up.

"Out into the cold again," he said, getting to his feet.

Maicy stood, too, waiting while he put his coat on again and then walking with him to the door.

Where he grabbed her, pulled her into his arms again and kissed her as if she was his to kiss before he ended it this time.

"Jane said that there's a dance tomorrow night in the school gym to get people out and celebrate the end of the town being blocked off," he said then. "Let's go."

Maicy made a face. "I don't know…"

"Come on. I'll be your shield against whatever comes your way."

She laughed. He was big enough to be a pretty good one.

"We've been even more cooped up than anyone around here. We deserve it. And if anybody should be hiding out in shame it should be Gary and Candace— you should be holding your head up high."

None of that persuaded her.

What did was the excuse of being with Conor.

He kissed her again and then she heard herself say, "Okay."

That made him smile and her drown in the glory of that face and those eyes of his. "Good," he said. "Charge your phone and I'll let you know tomorrow what happens with your car and what time I'll pick you up for the dance."

Maicy nodded, didn't reject yet another kiss and then watched him walk out the door.

Leaving her in the blast of cold air, knowing she was playing with fire.

Chapter Eight

"Gary…"

"Hi, Maicy…"

Alone in the minister's guesthouse on Saturday morning, Maicy had done a lot of pacing, dreading this very conversation but knowing it needed to happen.

Running away from the wedding had effectively canceled their planned commitment, but it hadn't canceled the relationship they'd had. She couldn't just leave things the way they were. There needed to be closure of some kind. And on a purely practical level, there were details that had to be sorted through about what to do with his belongings at her house in Denver, and—most important to Maicy—the fact that since she'd opted to use her grandmother's wedding ring as her own, Gary still had it and she needed that back.

So after fretting over it all, she'd finally shored up her courage and texted Gary.

We should talk. And I need the ring.

Gary had not responded.

But now it was midafternoon and here he was at her door.

"Did you get my text?" she asked flatly.

He pulled the ring box out of his pocket and handed it to her. "Can I come in?"

Maicy stepped out of the doorway so he could enter.

He was a not-terribly-tall, boyishly attractive man of slight build, with pale brown hair. And he couldn't hold a candle to Conor's swarthy good looks or the masculine, imposing presence that commanded any room.

Gary had come up short by comparison when they were all teenagers, and now? He definitely came up short now as he took off his coat.

After meticulously folding it and laying it over the arm of the sofa he looked at her, something sheepish in his plain brown eyes. "I'm sorry."

He'd been so involved in kissing his former girlfriend at the wedding that Maicy hadn't been sure if he was aware that he'd been caught—though perhaps the photographer had clued him in once he'd detached his tongue from his ex's tonsils.

She raised her chin at him but didn't say anything, wondering what exactly he was apologizing for.

"I know you saw us…Candace and me…kissing…"

So that *was* the reason for the apology.

"I don't know how long you were there," he went on. "But when you grabbed the cake box and ran out…"

Had they been making out a long time before that? Maicy wondered.

But she discovered that it didn't really matter to

her. Because standing there, looking at this man she'd almost married, her dominant emotions were still relief that she *hadn't* married him, and true certainty that they shouldn't have ever gotten engaged in the first place.

"I want you to know," he was saying, "that I haven't let you take the rap for the wedding not happening. I didn't tell anybody that you ran out. I said that we talked and both decided that maybe we didn't want to go through with it—"

"So you also didn't own up to what you did," she pointed out without rancor, just glad that while it was still embarrassing, she might not be in line for any scorn.

"I didn't, but…" He hesitated and she could see clearly that he didn't want to say what he was about to. But he did anyway. "Candace and I are back together so… Well, everybody knows that by now, and people are figuring that—"

"You dumped me for her," Maicy finished for him.

He shrugged, looking spineless to her.

"Basically that *is* what you did, I guess." But she'd been thinking more about her own actions and running out on the wedding and having to answer for that.

"It isn't that I *dumped* you… What happened with Candace just…happened. It took us both by surprise. Sparks flew and…"

Sparks…

Maicy had more of an understanding of that than she wished she did. Sparks were definitely flying with Conor no matter how hard she tried to douse or ignore them.

And here she was thinking about Conor even as Gary was talking.

She refocused on him but it took some effort.

"Candace realized that she'd turned me down because she'd been afraid, not because she didn't love me and…" He cut himself off, likely before saying that he loved Candace, too.

"I do care for you, Maicy," he continued when he'd regrouped. "When you and I met in Denver…it was like a little piece of home—comfortable and nice. And it was so easy to be with you."

That's what he'd been to her, too—comfortable, easy, uncomplicated. "But that isn't a reason to get married—for comfort," she contributed. She might have believed that before, but not anymore.

"And I think maybe there was some of that in it for you, too," he said tentatively.

She hadn't thought he'd realized how lukewarm her feelings for him were but she didn't deny it now. "I guess it's just a good thing you and Candace met up again *before* we got to the altar," she said.

"I'm staying in Northbridge," he confessed then. "I'm going back to working in my dad's accounting office. You know I didn't do well in Denver. I guess I'm not a city boy. But I'm really, really sorry for the way things ended…"

"Don't be," she said, meaning it. How could she fault him too much after what had been happening between her and Conor?

"I'll pay you back for what you spent on the wedding. It'll have to be in installments, but—"

Maicy shrugged that off, feeling a bit guilty for having accepted his proposal in the first place when she'd known her feelings for him weren't strong enough for marriage. If the price she had to pay was covering the cost of the failed wedding, she could live with that. "Do you want to come to Denver to get your things or—"

"If I never set eyes on Denver again it'll be okay with me. Could you pack them up and ship them to me? I'll pay for that, too, of course."

"Sure," Maicy said, fine with the prospect of not having him at her house again.

"So are we okay?" he asked then.

"We are," she answered, happy to have this behind her.

With nothing more to say, Gary put his coat back on, buttoning it up. "I heard it was Conor Madison at the Dales' cabin with you. Did you patch things up with him?"

The idea clearly didn't cause any more jealousy in Gary than the thought of him with Candace had caused in Maicy.

We really weren't meant for each other, she thought.

"I don't know that I'd say we *patched* anything up. But we did find some…middle ground, maybe."

"It'd be something if the two of you got back together, too, wouldn't it?"

"That's never going to happen," she said. Maybe too quickly. Too forcefully. She and Conor *weren't* going to get back together, she insisted to herself. Regardless of the sparks, regardless of whatever it was they were doing, *that* wasn't going to happen. She wasn't letting her guard down *that* far.

"Well, I only wish you the best, Maicy," Gary said then.

"You, too," she responded.

He stayed looking at her for another moment, smiling the smile of someone saying goodbye to an old friend.

"Thanks for everything you did for me—giving me a place to live, trying to find me a job...everything," he added.

Especially for running out on the wedding...

It was something that went through Maicy's mind as if he'd said it and made her smile a little, too.

"Sure," she said, walking with him to the door to let him out.

Once he was gone, once the awkward meeting was over, she breathed a genuine sigh of relief—thinking that sometimes things worked out the way they were supposed to.

For Gary and Candace.

There was no way she would put Conor rescuing her into that category.

Even if she did suddenly have the oddest sense that she was a little freer to go to that dance tonight with him.

Free enough to look forward to it.

A lot.

And maybe a little freer to have what everything in her had been crying out for since she'd made him stop last night...

Maicy had arrived in Northbridge only two days before her wedding and had been swept into last-minute details and preparations. In the course of that she'd encountered several people she'd known before, but not so many that being in the small town again had had the air of a reunion. The end-of-the-storm dance did.

It was held in the hastily decorated high school gym and included a potluck dinner to go along with dancing to the music of a local garage band that sometimes played at the town's single bar.

When she and Conor stepped into the doorway of the gym Maicy was met with a better reception than she'd feared. Someone good-naturedly shouted, "It's our runaway bride!"

So much for Gary thinking he'd convinced anyone that they'd just reached an amicable parting, Maicy thought. She shouldn't have believed that anything got past the eyes and ears of Northbridge.

But still everyone laughed at the runaway bride greeting, there was some applause and many shouts of "Welcome back!" and Maicy decided the best thing to do was play along. So she smiled and took a theatrical bow.

And that was it. From then on the incident seemed to be forgotten and the reunion-like air prevailed, making the evening fun.

It didn't even bother Maicy that Gary and Candace came with his family. She was reasonably sure that being there herself with Conor made all the difference in that. And while there were a few comments along the lines of Maicy-and-Conor-back-together-again, they both sidestepped them.

They shared a table with Rickie—who had to use two chairs so he could elevate his broken leg on one of them—and his family, including wife, Jane, and his three kids.

Jane doted on her husband in a way that made it clear that her long-ago crush on Conor was just that—long-ago and over with—so that didn't prove uncomfortable. Plus there was an endless stream of interruptions as people came to say hello and catch up with Maicy and with Conor.

And there was dancing.

Though Maicy did not dance with Conor.

On the way into the school she'd told him that she didn't want there to be anything between them that would set tongues wagging tonight and Conor honored that. They kept a friendly distance from each other, just two single people attending the same function. There weren't any romantic overtures or any exchanges of private conversation. Maicy didn't even pay strict attention when he told Rickie and Jane the things that he'd told her on the way to the dance—that he had been able to speak directly to his brother and while Declan was still very ill, the antibiotics were helping. That Declan had insisted that since Conor had come all this way already, he should go to Denver to at least spend a day with their sister before he returned to Declan's bedside.

She'd also left it to Conor to tell them that both of their vehicles had been dug out of the snow and brought to the farm, where the local mechanic had gone to check them out. That the rental SUV was fine but Maicy's accident had left her car in need of a part the mechanic didn't have. The mechanic had done a temporary fix that he wasn't sure would hold to get Maicy all the way to Denver. But he'd shown Conor how to redo the fix if it failed, so Conor was going to follow her in his rental to make sure she made it safely before seeing his sister. And not even through all of that did he speak directly to her, so everything seemed completely innocent.

Until the last dance.

Just as the band announced it, Maicy's high school frog-dissecting-partner stepped up to ask for his second dance of the night, and Conor inserted himself between him and Maicy.

He was friendly but firm when he said, "Sorry, this one is all mine." Then he held out his hand to her. And she didn't hesitate before accepting it. Despite the ground rules she'd laid down as they'd arrived tonight, she'd spent every minute of what had turned out to be a pleasant event regretting the rules she'd put in place between them. Wishing with everything in her that he would just fold her into his arms and let her have him all to herself.

Which was what finally happened on the dance floor.

Except that he stood military-straight and tall and stiff, and held her at a respectable distance that felt as if there was still a mile between them.

But at least dancing gave her the excuse to focus solely on him, on the fine features of his face, to peer up into cobalt blue eyes that looked at her in a way no one else ever had.

Even as he smiled blandly and said for her ears only, "This is killing me."

Maicy laughed. "What is?"

"You know what is—acting like I hardly know you're here, watching you dance with other guys, keeping my hands off you…" His hand at her waist and the one that held hers both gripped her more firmly— something she felt but no one would be able to see.

"Tonight has been nice, though," she said as if she hadn't been going out of her mind wanting more of him. "It's almost made me sorry that I haven't been back to visit here until now. That I didn't stay in touch with anyone. I've actually been feeling a little homesick for Northbridge tonight."

"You could move back," he suggested.

Maicy laughed. "I wouldn't go that far. But who knows, I might not skip the next class reunion."

"Surprisingly, I made it to mine. I just happened to be on leave and visiting my folks when it happened. But you skipped yours?"

"Oh, yeah."

"You didn't just skip it, you avoided it like the plague," he guessed from her tone.

"They couldn't have paid me to come," she confirmed.

"Why? You never hated Northbridge—in fact, back when you proposed, you said that we could have a good life here if we stayed instead of heading to college."

"I believed that," she said. "But then you left and that last year here, after losing my mom...you..." she added quietly, "all I wanted was to put this place behind me and never look back, and that's what I did. I guess the same way I chose to forget that we'd ever had anything good together before the split, I forgot that there was anything good about Northbridge, too. Tonight I remembered, though—it's not a bad place and neither are the people in it. I was happy here before things fell apart."

"Think you would have been happy if you'd stayed?" he asked.

"Not then." Because she honestly didn't think she would have been happy in the small town without him. But she wasn't willing to say that.

Conor nodded as if he understood anyway. "A lot of people have stayed," he said, taking his eyes off her to glance around the gym before his attention was all on her once more. "They married, had kids… Hard for me to imagine some of the couple combinations that have happened over the years. Harder still to see some of these guys as parents—"

"Rickie especially—I know," Maicy agreed with another laugh. "He was such a—"

"Screw-up," Conor finished with a laugh of his own.

"And now he has your Jane and two *teenagers*—"

"She was not *my* Jane," Conor corrected before he seemed to become more reflective and said, "I keep thinking what if…what if we'd stayed."

"Yeah, me, too," Maicy said. "But what would we have done?" she reasoned, echoing his arguments from eighteen years ago. "You wanted to be a doctor from long before you and I ever got together—and you couldn't have done that here. I know you hated working on the farm. If that was what you'd ended up doing you wouldn't have been happy. And the military…your stepfather had you and Liam and Declan in that mindset when you were all still in elementary school. There was no question about you all joining the service."

"Yeah, that's all true," he said but with a hint of regret in his voice. "And what about you? You were talking about skipping college—which would have been a waste of that brain of yours. What would you have done here?"

Maicy shrugged at the question. "You were right back then. I would have done just any old dead-end job that I would likely have hated. It took leaving here to learn how to take care of myself, to get me where I am—and I like where I am. I don't think I would have had that same determination if we had stayed."

"Plus there would have probably been kids..."

"It would have been a different life." Maybe better in some ways, worse in others, but definitely different.

Perhaps Conor was thinking the same thing because he only said, "Yeah..."

He pulled her closer—not a lot, just enough to rest his chin on the top of her head. But something about it felt possessive. "I have to tell you, though, I look at Rickie and I'm kind of jealous—"

"You *did* want Jane," Maicy accused, obviously joking.

"No. But I am jealous that he's not going home alone tonight..."

She laughed yet again. "That was not subtle."

He chuckled. "I'm not feeling like there's time for subtlety," he admitted. "What I *am* feeling is that I've spent this whole damn day hating that last night ended and wanting to pick up where we left off."

That was exactly what she'd been feeling.

But before she could say anything, Conor took her elbows and lifted them so that both of her arms were around his neck. Then he locked his hands at the small of her back and looked down at her again in a way that made everything else recede, leaving Maicy with the sense that they were alone in the room.

"I'm just thinking that your car is at my place, that by now the minister and his family are long asleep," he said softly. "We could pack up your things at the guesthouse, slip a thank-you and the key under the main house's door, and you could come with me out to the farm tonight instead of having someone bring you out in the morning. We could have tonight together before we head for Denver tomorrow. Because once we hit Denver tomorrow," he mused, "this is all going to end. You're going back to your life. I'm going back to mine..." He breathed a warm gust of air into her hair before he whispered, "But here we are now..." He paused, then said even more softly, "Give me tonight, Maicy..."

She didn't mean for it to happen but as she thought about that her cheek went to his chest and keeping up appearances was forgotten as she considered going home with him.

She'd been worried last night that she'd wanted him to make love to her *too* much. That she might make the decision in the heat of the moment and regret it afterward.

But this wasn't the heat of the moment.

And they wouldn't be in the minister's guesthouse.

Conor was suggesting that they slip away to his place in the country, where they could have this one last night alone before they rejoined the real world and their real lives.

As she thought about it, she realized that she didn't actually have to ask herself if she would regret making love with Conor because she knew she wouldn't. Instead it suddenly seemed like the natural course of things.

He was supposed to have been her first. But that wasn't what happened. And while, over the years, there had been a part of her that had been glad that she hadn't given up her virginity to someone who had disillusioned and disappointed her so resoundingly, there was another part of her that had regretted that she hadn't. And it had most definitely left her wondering.

Now maybe fate was not only giving her the opportunity to sort through some of the past with Conor, but also the opportunity to know him in the one way that she'd never gotten to explore. The one thing she'd wanted desperately and denied herself.

The one thing she wanted desperately all over again.

And she *did* want him desperately. Not because of the relationship they'd had years ago, but because of the man he was now. The adult Conor she'd discovered herself attracted to in spite of their past, even as she'd fought her attraction.

Tonight, she didn't want to say no. Instead, she wanted this man. The man he was now. Knowing full well that it would only be this one time.

That thought gave her a pretty severe twinge. But she ignored it. She wanted to get back to her life, there was no doubt about that. But before that happened, she also wanted this one last night with Conor, both to put the past to rest and more, to satisfy what the adult Conor had brought to life in her now. And after last night she knew that if she *didn't* go home with him tonight, it was *that* that she would really regret. Forever.

The music ended just then and so did their dance.

Maicy took her head off his chest and gazed up at his face again, drinking in the sight of him.

"What about that 'no exertion because of my head injury' thing?" she teased.

He grinned and that only made him all the sexier. "You can let me do all the work," he answered without skipping a beat, a sly sparkle in those blue eyes.

She laughed once more, paused just to bask in the way he looked at her again, and then said, "Okay."

His grin got bigger, he clasped one of her hands in his and didn't bother to say good-night to anyone, taking her out of the gym, bypassing everyone in the lobby and grabbing their coats to get her out of the school and to his SUV.

Neither of them said much as they returned to the guesthouse, made short work of getting her things and enacted his thank-you-note-and-key-slipped-under-the-door plan.

Neither of them said much as they drove out of town and headed for the farm. But the silence was both peaceful and charged with an underlying excitement. In an odd way, she felt like she was heading for the wedding night she'd always fantasized about. The wedding night that she'd been sure she'd share with Conor, that would make the waiting worthwhile.

When they pulled up in front of the farmhouse she was only vaguely aware that it looked the same as it always had. Her attention was on Conor taking her suitcase from his back seat as she got out of the SUV.

And then they went inside.

He closed the door after them and dropped the suitcase where he stood so he could spin her around to him and catch her mouth with his. But they weren't really picking up where they'd left off the night before because while Maicy had expected a blitz kind of kiss, this was soft and slow and sweet. The kind of kiss that savored that initial meeting of his mouth and hers.

Still, it did the trick. For Maicy, in that moment, the world was shut out and everything fell away so that she could give herself over to everything she'd been wanting.

Making almost no contact, Conor took off her wool coat, letting that drop to the floor, too, before he shrugged out of his and discarded it the same way.

His hands came to the sides of her face then, keeping her in that kiss as it deepened and grew more intense.

Then he stopped, clasped her hand in his and led her up the stairs.

"Upstairs was off-limits," she whispered as if they weren't there alone.

"Not anymore," he said with a smile he cast over his shoulder at her as she took in the very fine sight of him from behind.

When they reached the upper level he brought her into the second bedroom, plain and simple with only a double bed, nightstands and a bureau to furnish it.

"Was this your room?" she asked.

"Back in the day. Now all of our rooms are guest rooms. Mom didn't want to keep the posters or the military and sport stuff, I guess," he said affectionately. "You've been here before…" He swung her around to face him again, his hands at the small of her back. "But only in pictures. And in my fantasies," he added, his smile stretching into a wicked grin before he kissed her again, this one not so slow or soft or sweet, but with lips parted from the start and a wicked tongue coming to dare her to play.

It was a dare Maicy took. He'd worn jeans and a quarter-zip mock-neck sweater tonight, leaving the zipper partially down to expose his throat. It was the open ends of that sweater that she grasped, pulling him into that kiss even further and letting her own tongue introduce so much simmering sensuality that she even surprised herself.

It wasn't lost on him because she heard a quiet rumble in his throat and his arms tightened around her, bringing his hands into a firm hold of her back through the dark gray silk blouse she'd worn tonight with black slacks.

She went on kissing him with the seductiveness of a siren as she kicked off her shoes.

The two-inch-lower height gave him a bit of an advantage that he took, turning the kiss into something more fevered and hungry.

Maicy let go of his collar and lowered the zipper of his sweater. Then she ended that kiss to press her lips to his chest at the lowest point of the sweater's opening.

He laughed, got rid of his own shoes, then let out a sort of growl and swooped her into his arms to lay her on the bed.

Still standing at the foot of it himself, he yanked his sweater off over his head and threw it aside with a vengeance.

The curtains on the two windows in the room were open. Moonlight reflected off the snow, leaving the space bathed in a white glow brighter than any candlelight, and letting Maicy see for sure that there was a vast improvement in Conor-the-man's bare chest over what Conor-the-boy's had been.

He was all broad shoulders and honed muscles that she couldn't wait to get her hands on, so she was glad that he didn't hesitate to join her on the bed.

Straddling her legs, he knee-walked to her hips, his cobalt blue eyes locked on hers as he reached for the buttons of her blouse and began to unfasten them, slowly exposing the lacy black demi-cup bra she'd worn tonight.

He must have liked it because when he slid her blouse off, he stole a glance and gave a little groan of appreciation. The kind of appreciation Maicy volleyed back when she laid her hands to his flat stomach and slid them up his superb torso.

About the time she reached his shoulders he dipped down to kiss her again, a leisurely and oh-so-sexy kiss that locked them together as he stretched out next to her and rolled her with him so they were both on their sides, where he draped one leg over her to pull her up against him.

There were still too many clothes between their bottom halves, though...

That brought memories of make-out sessions of yore when despite exploring hands and the intimate press of bodies, clothes had remained on.

To distract herself from it Maicy focused on that kiss, on the feel of the bare skin she could reach, running her hands from his waistband up the widening V of his back, digging her fingers into the span of his shoulders, feeling the flex of those muscles beneath her touch, and learning the iron strength of impressive biceps before she tested to see what kind of reaction she got from massaging pectorals with slightly taut nibs at their centers.

Slightly taut. Nothing at all like her own nipples that were little diamonds straining for his touch as one of his hands came around from her back to cup a breast in his palm.

Maicy couldn't suppress a sigh at the feel of it, especially when he did something he'd never done before and unhooked her bra, tossing it aside. Leaving her something she'd never been with him before—topless.

Her arousal deepened, intensified, causing her breasts to swell into the hand that was again working magic, kneading and caressing and tantalizing each globe in turn.

For a bit, anyway, until he stopped kissing her, nudged her to her back and found one breast with his mouth while his hand went on tormenting the other, raising the stakes and her yearning along with them.

Oh that mouth and tongue and teeth...

He knew what to do with them all and drove her wild, sucking and flicking and circling and tugging her to distraction until she could barely keep from writhing.

And she couldn't stop herself from finding the button fly of jeans when everything in her demanded more of him.

She closed her hand around him, long and thick and strong and as impressive as the rest of him, and felt his grip on her breast tighten in response to his own pleasure even as he groaned his approval and she put some effort into driving him a little crazy.

A new urgency came over him with that, and before long he got off the bed again, pulling Maicy by the ankles to the end, where he took off her slacks, spent a moment admiring her black lace bikini panties before he slipped those off, too, reveling in the sight of her naked body.

"Oh yeah..." he breathed.

He took a condom from his jean pocket, then dropped his jeans and boxers, and put the condom on while Maicy ogled the magnificence of him that was far greater than anything she'd ever imagined. And something she wanted to know every inch of by touch.

When he came back onto the bed he kissed her again with an all-new fervor, clearly equally eager to explore because as her hands left nothing of him unknown, his traveled everywhere on her, gliding over her skin, sending all inhibitions fleeing, making her pliable and willing before his hand again sought her breasts.

But only for a while before his mouth did, too, freeing his hand to sluice lower, between her legs and into her for a teaser that only drove them both into even more of a frenzy that had to have an outlet.

He nudged her knees apart and rose up over her to find his place between them. To slide smoothly into her.

She never wanted to think that she needed any man to complete her. And yet the moment he was inside of her that *was* how she felt.

Her muscles contracted around him all on their own, holding tight. And she knew he felt it because he moaned with pleasure and surprise and revelation all at once, and he pushed in farther still before establishing a rhythm in and out that Maicy met and matched, her arms around his expansive back holding tight, her thighs and hips aiding the cause.

They moved together and apart, together and apart in unison, both of them striving in answer to what was building, growing between them. Until it reached a peak that exploded in Maicy first and arched her up off the mattress, a high-pitched moan of ecstasy escaping from her just as she felt Conor reach a peak of his own.

Every inch of him stiffened and he plunged even deeper into her as she clung to him, curling her legs around his and pulling him deeper still, their bodies seamlessly together as he brought her to a second, even more powerful crest that was so incredible she tried not to let it pass.

But it did anyway. Slowly releasing her from its hold until they were both drained and spent and collapsed a little.

And once again she was aware of the feel of him inside of her and the thought ran through her mind that she never wanted him anywhere else.

But she chased that thought away and merely enjoyed the weight of him on top of her while they both caught their breath.

Still joined, he wrapped her in his arms and legs and rolled them to their sides again, where he held her close.

He pressed a lingering kiss to the top of her head, sighed a replete sigh, and said, "Are you all right?"

She laughed at the concern in his tone, knowing that now that the deed was done he was worrying about her health again. "Never better," she assured.

"No headache?"

"I did see stars…" she teased, making him laugh.

"You're welcome," he said cockily.

"So are you," she countered, not to be outdone.

"Oh, believe me, I'm grateful," he said, pulsing inside of her.

Then all at once he let go of her and disappeared into what she assumed was a bathroom, before he came back and settled again beside her, pulling her as close as he could get her—only this time he yanked one side of the quilt over them, binding them together.

"Sleep," he ordered. "You need rest."

That was true enough—like with every exertion since the accident, she had tired out faster than normal. But she was loath to close her eyes and miss any of what felt so perfect at that moment.

It was actually Conor who fell asleep before she did, still keeping her near even then, nestled in his arms in a way that was again so, so much better than she'd ever known it could be.

But despite wanting to stay awake and revel in it, she couldn't fight off sleep for long.

And as she began to lose that battle, it occurred to her that the other thing she couldn't fight off was an ache at the thought that this wasn't for forever...

Chapter Nine

It took fourteen hours to make the eight-hour drive from Northbridge to Denver on Sunday. The highway varied from clear to snow-packed, and stopping for checks on the temporary repair of Maicy's engine slowed their progress, too.

The short-term fix lasted, though, all the way to Maicy's mechanic—Rob, the nineteen-year-old brother of her friend Rachel.

Rob either had a crush on Maicy or orders from his sister to rescue her from Conor because he all but shoved Conor out of the way to get to her the minute they arrived at the shop where he worked.

And once he had, he said he would take over from there—both with the car and with getting Maicy home. Then he hovered like a bodyguard, allowing them nothing more than a scant goodbye before insisting that

Maicy come with him to discuss what the car needed. Leaving Conor with no recourse but to watch her be taken from him as she called a thank-you to him over her shoulder.

And that was it.

But how the hell could that be?

That was what kept screaming through Conor's brain even as he called his sister to tell her he was minutes away from her apartment. Even as he called to check on Declan—asleep but still stable. And even through meeting his sister's fiancé Sutter Knightlinger before he dropped his gear in Kinsey's guest room and took a shower.

It was still screaming through his brain as he left the guest room to find his sister saying the kind of heated, passionate goodbye to Sutter that he wished he'd been able to say to Maicy.

Damn, this just wasn't how their time together should end…

"I made a roast for dinner in case you got home earlier." Kinsey's enthusiastic voice cut through his thoughts when her fiancé tossed Conor a good-night and left. "But since it's almost nine o'clock, how about a roast beef sandwich? I've got tomatoes and lettuce and a Havarti cheese with dill in it that'll be great on it!"

"Sure. Okay," he answered her.

"Come and sit at the table while I fix it. Can I get you a beer?"

"Yeah, a beer would be great." He made himself focus on his sister, fighting to clear his head as he nodded in the direction of the apartment door. "Sutter seems like a good guy."

"The best!" she corrected, going on to effusively tell him all the ways in which her fiancé excelled until Conor laughed and cried uncle against the onslaught.

"I get it, I get it—you like him," he understated.

"Oh, sooo much…"

"It's a good thing since you're marrying him. I'm just glad he makes you happy. And that you aren't lonely anymore. You aren't, right?" He knew loneliness was part of what had prompted her to pursue the Camden connection.

"Not lonely, no," she said, adding in a warning tone, "But I still want family, Conor."

"You have family—Declan, Liam and me, and in a few months Sutter and his mother. Then probably kids." It was something he'd said to her before and she was no more receptive to it now than she had been previously.

"I—*we*—also have four half brothers and two half sisters, nieces, nephews, cousins and a *grandmother*," she persisted. "A grandmother, Conor—none of us were born in time to know grandparents on Mom's side, and here we are, with a living breathing one just blocks away from this very spot! How can you not want to know her? Or the rest of them?"

"It isn't that I wouldn't want to know them under other circumstances, Kins. But as it is we're their father's bastard secret family. Our mother—"

"Don't say it!" She stopped him. "You always try to scare me off this by focusing on the worst thing they might say about her. I know you do it for shock value but it doesn't change the way I feel. These people are our flesh and blood. Georgianna Camden is as fully our grandmother as she is to all ten of the others, and I want them to be a part of my life."

"They aren't rushing in for that," he reminded her. "They're having us investigated like we're some kind of scam artists or lowlifes."

"In their position they have to be careful," she defended. "And so what if they're investigating us? All they can find is that it's the truth."

"And then what, Kins? Truth or not, it doesn't change how they feel about the whole thing, about us. About Mom. Do you really want family that hates or resents us?"

"I'm hoping for the best," his sister said stubbornly. "And you should know that I'm inviting every one of them to the wedding—the side of the family that Sutter is related to, and the side we're related to, along with our grandmother."

Conor shook his head. "We're just afraid you're setting yourself up for a fall," he said, speaking for his brothers as well as himself.

"I can take it," she claimed. "Especially now that I have Sutter. But I'd like for you and Liam and Declan to be on board, too," she added hopefully.

"I...I don't know what to tell you, Kins... None of us are going to be on board with mud being slung at Mom—you have to know that."

"I wouldn't stand for that, either. But I've met these people and that isn't how they are. They're good, decent people—"

"The Camdens haven't always been good, decent people," he pointed out. "You know the reputation of the ones who died in that crash—ruthless, underhanded, willing to do *anything* to get what they wanted, to get all they have now. And if Mitchum Camden had been good or decent he wouldn't have cheated on his wife, on his family. He wouldn't have put Mom in the position she was in or had a whole second family on the side. It was Hugh who married Mom and took us on and treated us as his own—*that's* a good, decent guy."

Then he realized he'd been practically shouting. Okay, maybe he needed to tone it down for his sister's sake. What he and his brothers said to each other on this subject might be too harsh for Kinsey, who genuinely wanted to be a part of the Camden family.

She finished making his sandwich and brought it to him, sitting in the chair across from him at the small round kitchen table.

"Mom loved him," she said simply. "She was ashamed of being the *other woman*, embarrassed. She never wanted his wife, his other family, to know about her or us because she didn't want to hurt any of them. But even though she knew it was wrong, she couldn't change the way she felt. She said she wished she hadn't loved him, that she tried to stop and so did he. But neither of them could."

After what he'd felt during this last week with Maicy, much of that struck home for Conor and he didn't have a comeback for it. So all he said was, "I guess we'll just have to see what happens. We just don't want you to get hurt if they aren't interested in connecting. Because you know that could happen—it kind of already did when you showed the grandmother the letter that Mom left us explaining this whole thing."

"And that was hard," Kinsey admitted. "But I came out of their house to Sutter and he was like a safety net, waiting there, ready to cushion the blow. So like I said, having him will help if the Camdens never come around to accepting us, and you guys don't have to worry as much about it not working out. For the first time since you all left home and joined the military, I'm not alone in whatever happens."

"I'm sorry that you have been, Kinsey. So are Liam and Declan. We know finding out about this might have had a different impact on you if we'd been here to help out over the years."

"I'm counting Sutter as my reward for the sacrifices, so you can all stop feeling guilty for that. But I still like the idea of a big family, here, around me. Including a grandmother who can become great-grandmother to my kids. So I'm not giving up on the Camdens and I think they're going to surprise you."

"For your sake, I hope you're right," he said with the full extent of his doubts in his tone.

"And when I make out the wedding invitations," his sister said coyly then, "should I send one to Maicy? Or maybe she'll be your plus-one if you make it home…"

The first thing Conor and Kinsey had discussed when he'd arrived had been Declan's health, so Kinsey had already had the update on their brother. Conor hadn't been too forthcoming with his sister about his career conundrum, so she didn't know how much that was weighing on him. But of course the fact that he'd just spent a week in a secluded cabin with his old high school sweetheart would intrigue Kinsey even though she hadn't gotten around to the subject until now. Though she'd been several years younger, too young to be close to Maicy when Conor had been dating her, Kinsey had always liked Maicy. And had seen what he'd gone through when she'd dumped him.

"Oh, no… I don't know…that all seems weird…" he answered, struggling for something that would make sense. Then he settled on, "Nothing's changed just because we were snowed in."

That wasn't true—everything had changed. But now that they'd made it to Denver, everything needed to change back as they returned to their regularly scheduled lives, which didn't include each other.

"Come on, it's me you're talking to. I know how you were about her," his sister said with some authority.

It was authority she'd earned because while he'd put on a brave front eighteen years ago for their tough-as-nails stepfather, and for Declan and Liam, he'd shown some of his feelings over the breakup to his mother and shared even more of them with Kinsey.

"That was almost two decades ago," he said, dodging the issue.

"And now you've just had more than a week with her—most of it *alone* with her. Don't tell me it didn't stir up old feelings."

Old ones. New ones.

Feelings that kept shouting that this just wasn't how their time together should end.

"I don't know, Kins—" he said yet again.

But he was literally saved by the bell just then because his sister's cell phone rang and when she looked at the display she said, "This is Sutter... His mother, the colonel, has bronchitis and—"

"Answer it," Conor encouraged.

She did, leaving him to eat while she had a brief conversation with her fiancé about his mother. It concluded with her saying she would come right over.

Then she ended the call and made a guilt-ridden face at Conor. "I have to go check on her," she said.

Conor laughed. "This is a switch, isn't it? Usually

when one of us comes to see you, you make time stand still for the visit. Now it's you who has something else calling you away."

"I'm sorry."

"Don't be. How many times have we left you hanging? I'm just glad to see your life full enough to have priorities outside of us. Do you want backup?" he offered.

"The colonel saw her doctor yesterday—that's who diagnosed the bronchitis. So I don't think she needs a doctor right now. It sounds like she just needs a nebulizer treatment. But if that isn't enough I'll call you. And I'll be back as soon as I can—we can sit up all night talking."

As much as he loved and missed his sister, it was Maicy he would really like to have the prospect of that with. Although maybe not for *only* talking...

"Don't worry about it," he told his sister. "If you need to stay over there for the night to keep an eye on things, go ahead. The monster storm moved east and now Maryland is socked in with it and their airports are closed. Thank God Declan is doing better because I'll be lucky to get back to him by Tuesday, but that means you and I will still have at least tomorrow to catch up."

"You're sure?" Kinsey said.

"I am. Duty calls—and so do the other people in your life now—so stay there and take care of them. After all the driving I did today, it's better if I just sack out anyway."

"I probably should monitor the colonel's breathing overnight..."

"Go!" Conor commanded.

She did, leaving him alone with the remainder of his sandwich and his thoughts.

Thoughts that were *not* about going to sleep. That instead were all about Maicy and how he was almost glad to have his sister leave so he might have the chance yet tonight to maybe call her or text her. Something. Anything.

To say a proper goodbye to her—that was what he told himself he was contemplating doing.

But was that really what he was aiming for? Just to say the goodbye the mechanic hadn't allowed? For closure for what had opened up between them since the snowstorm had thrown them together?

Yeah, that *should* have been what he was aiming for.

But instead, he was just thinking about how much he wanted to talk to her, to see her. Last night had been better than anything he'd ever fantasized about, better than everything he'd ever imagined it might be. And it had unleashed something in him. He'd thought that if they never left that bed, he could be a happy man.

They'd only made love once and there was no way once had been enough for him. But he'd forced himself to keep in mind that Maicy was still recovering from the accident, that they had the drive to Denver to make, that she needed to sleep. So he'd let her. Snuggled to his side, her head on his chest, one naked thigh over his, his arms around her.

But four times he'd woken up just to reassure himself that she was honestly there. Wanting her so damn bad again. Having to remind himself that he *had* to let her rest, even as he'd basked in her being in his bed, in his arms, where he'd wanted her since he was seventeen.

Their plan had been to get up at dawn and head for Denver. And as was his way, he'd stuck to his plan despite everything in him demanding that he keep her there and make love to her again. But he'd used every drop of willpower his stepfather and the navy had ever drilled into him, and he'd gotten out of that bed.

He'd kept her in his sights through the entire drive from Northbridge, not really thinking about losing her again once the drive was over because it didn't seem—hadn't seemed all through the drive—like that was a possibility. Not after last night.

That had been shortsighted of him. They'd already discussed how getting out of Northbridge had been the cutoff to what was happening between them. The end. The time when they both went back to their separate lives.

But then last night had happened and…

And gut-punched him.

Last night had been more than unfinished business or any kind of ending.

Last night had seemed like a new beginning…

He stood up from his sister's table and took his beer and his plate with him. He rinsed the plate and put it in the dishwasher, then took a swig of beer as he leaned against the counter's edge, still lost in thought.

But what kind of new beginning could last night be? he asked himself.

He was still the guy who had let Maicy down when she'd needed him most.

He still had to get to his brother to make sure Declan came through all right.

He was still in some kind of weird limbo over his

job—a job that would either take him away for long stints or one that would mean nearly starting over.

And Maicy was still where she'd ended up *because* he'd let her down—someone with a business of her own, with a life and friends that held her in Denver.

So what exactly was he thinking was a new beginning?

And a beginning of what?

He hadn't been *thinking*, he realized then. It was only a *sense* that there was a new beginning. It was only feelings that had him in their grip. Feelings about her.

He wanted her.

He wanted her as much now as he had years ago. More...

Yeah, he wanted to make love to her again. That was a given. But that wasn't all he wanted. He just wanted her.

When they were kids she'd been a pretty, good-natured, soft-hearted girl. Fun and funny and a little feisty. Sweet and uncomplicated.

But now?

Now she wasn't merely pretty, she was beautiful.

The soft-heartedness was still there—or she wouldn't have demanded that they save the mouse at the cabin, he thought with a laugh. And she was still fun and funny. But that feistiness had a touch of fire to it, a touch of stubbornness that only gave her personality more depth.

Depth she had all the way around now.

She was strong and resilient and confident. She was organized and efficient and more capable than she'd been as a girl. Braver, even. Brave enough to shoo away a mountain lion.

Thinking about that made him laugh again and realize how much he liked every bit of her. Every aspect just added to the intrigue of her. The sexiness of her. It all just made her one hell of a woman.

A woman who had not only provided a distraction from his concerns and frustrations over Declan but had talked him through them, calmed him.

And she'd been the perfect person to be stranded with. There hadn't been any whining or complaining about the conditions of the cabin, about any of the inconveniences. She hadn't milked the situation or her injury the way someone else might have. Instead she'd been determined to contribute, to do her share. She'd pushed through headaches and dizziness and weakness rather than giving in to them. And she was resourceful—it was Maicy who'd explored their options and devised the plan for how to move Rickie and get him into the truck while Conor had dealt with his friend's broken leg.

She just had so much more substance, so many more layers than she'd had before.

Much of which had come out of him hurting her.

And made it seem like he was the last person who should be in line to benefit from or enjoy any of it…

God, he wished he could wipe that slate clean!

And what if he could? he asked himself. What if they *could* have a new beginning? A future together?

What would that future look like?

Certainly, it would be different from anything he'd contemplated for a long time. It would require major deviations from the plan he'd made for himself. But the clock was ticking on making the decision about what path to take professionally. And that was the first thing he had to sort through...

Could he be satisfied with his life if he stayed in a job that frustrated him more every day? His successes in trauma medicine meant saving a life or a limb in a particular moment. That was something vital, but it was also without a sense of permanence, a sense of complete satisfaction, when he knew the patient had so much further to go before being home free, before they walked out of a hospital under their own steam or returned to their life.

Trauma medicine lacked deeper fulfillment. It was patch up and pass on.

He'd liked that when he'd first started out. It wasn't enough now but he was convinced that the navy wouldn't stand still for him changing his path.

So how to decide?

Take the military out of the equation.

That had been Maicy's advice. Maybe it was time he took it.

So what if he did factor out the military and only considered his medical career?

There was no appeal in doing another residency, a fellowship.

But there was even less appeal in the prospect of sticking with what he was doing now.

And between the two he suddenly knew that he would rather take a few years to step back and retrain than face thirty or forty more, frustrated and dissatisfied and discontent. That he would rather spend those few years in residency and fellowship and then be able to go on in a field he would ultimately prefer for the bulk of his career.

Which left him with one answer.

He had to leave the navy.

But accepting that was no easy task and he chugged the rest of his beer as he tried to sort through it.

Maicy had been right when she'd said that his stepfather had heavily encouraged him and his brothers to be career military. To serve until they were of no more use to their country. That was the plan.

But if changing his medical specialty altered his medical career plan without trashing it, was there a way to alter the plan to serve his country without giving it up entirely?

Looking at things in a clearer light now, he didn't need more than posing that question to find an answer.

He'd seen for himself how short-staffed veterans' hospitals were. If he went to work as a contract physician in a veterans' facility he would still be serving his country and repaying the military for his education, it would just be as a veteran himself rather than as active military.

It wasn't the original plan. It probably wouldn't have pleased Hugh. But it was a workable alternative.

A new plan.

A new plan thanks to Maicy's guidance.

And one load lifted off his shoulders.

Freeing him to think about what his new, civilian life might include. Like Maicy. After all, she *was* the whole reason he'd started thinking about this. As much as he wanted and needed a career change, he wanted and needed her even more. At any cost.

And now that he'd decided to reset his course, he had more to offer her.

An offer he needed to make because he didn't want to say goodbye to her. He didn't want to lose her again. He *couldn't* lose her again!

Maybe he'd been a stupid young fool not to say yes to her eighteen years ago, or maybe he hadn't—he honestly didn't know. But he did know at that moment that no matter what it took, he had to have her now.

If she'd have him...

God, that seemed like a big if.

Especially when he suddenly knew that he was in the position she'd been in eighteen years ago—she'd sorted through the crisis she'd been in the midst of, believed she'd found a solution for it, and had only needed him to say yes.

And he hadn't.

"It would serve you right if she kicked your ass out the door," he told himself.

And it terrified him like nothing in his life ever had that she might.

So what was he going to do?

There was a single answer to that.

He threw his beer bottle into the recycle bin, took his sister's spare apartment key from the hook she kept it on and headed for the door.

Because Maicy saying no was a chance he had to take.

Chapter Ten

"Um, Maicy, some guy just pulled up in front of your house. Some really hot guy..."

Rachel's brother Rob had driven Maicy home, where she'd taken a quick shower and shampoo, twisted her hair into a careless, lopsided knot, then dressed in a soft loungewear T-shirt and flannel pajama pants to go across the street to Rachel's house to have pizza with her friend and her friend's husband.

After eating, Jake had gone to the den to watch television and left Maicy and Rachel to talk and catch up. That was what they'd been doing for the last two hours, sitting in Rachel's living room.

Rachel was curled up on an overstuffed chair that gave her a view of Maicy's house through the front window behind the couch where Maicy was sitting.

"Who would come over this late?" Maicy responded

as she pivoted around to peer out the window, too. Then she said, "That's Conor!"

Whom they had talked extensively about tonight.

"What's he doing here?" she added as she watched him get out of his rented SUV.

"Booty call?" Rachel joked.

"I left my phone at home to charge. Do you think he called or texted? How'd he find me?"

"*Determination* for a booty call?" was Rachel's laughing response as she joined Maicy, kneeling on the sofa beside her to stare directly out the window. "He probably just looked up your address. Why are you sitting here? Go over there!" her friend urged.

Maicy wasn't so sure about that.

Last night with him had rattled her. It had been so good that all of her defenses had disintegrated, leaving her completely unguarded and vulnerable in ways she hadn't been since the day Conor had rejected her proposal. Ways that scared her to death.

Driving back to Denver she'd fought to resurrect everything that had protected her through the last eighteen years. She'd reminded herself in no uncertain terms that she was *not* the wide-eyed, trusting, naive young girl she'd once been. That she did *not* believe in fairy tales and that she had to take care of herself.

She'd told herself that regardless of how things had developed between her and Conor at the cabin, regardless of the support he'd offered in Northbridge and the rekindling of their former connection there, regardless of one mind-bogglingly incredible love-making session and sleeping in his arms more soundly than she'd ever slept before, it was over. Done. Finished. Sealed and filed away once and for all.

She'd actually texted Rachel during the last stop they'd made to check her engine on the way to Denver, asking her friend to alert Rob that she was on her way to his shop and get him to run interference between her and Conor. To do exactly what he'd done—save her from any long, lingering goodbyes between them.

It had been a safety precaution so she didn't give in to the temptation to ask Conor to spend tonight with her—something she knew he was bound to turn down in favor of time with his sister. Because of course his family would be prioritized over her.

Not that she *should* be anywhere on his list of priorities, she'd also reminded herself. But so many lines had been blurred and everything had somehow gotten so confusing and complicated...

"Maicy?" Rachel's voice interrupted her thoughts, sounding confused herself. "Are you going over there?"

Her heart was racing and no, she still wasn't eager to cross the street and be with him again. Why was he there, anyway? Just to say the long, lingering goodbye she'd already taken measures to avoid? To say a *thanks, it's been fun, maybe I'll see you again in eighteen or twenty years and we can have another go-round*?

Or maybe he really was just there for a booty call. But while last night had left her wanting a whole lot more intimacy with him, wanting it as much as she did was a warning that it was exactly what she *shouldn't* indulge in.

The plain truth was that he'd shaken her foundation again.

After he'd turned down her proposal it had taken her a long time to feel like she was standing on solid ground.

A longer time to build the solid base that she'd erected for herself and evolve into the person she was now.

One week with him—including one night in bed with him—and things were suddenly wobbly again.

And coming from that weak-kneed position, she was worried that she might once more be helpless when it came to her attraction to him, that she was just too susceptible to him.

And where would that leave her when he was gone again? Wanting things he wasn't going to give her? Hating herself for it? Hating him again? Angry and hurt and in a state of mind she never, ever wanted to revisit?

"Hey," her friend said, nudging her arm to jar her out of her reverie. "It's okay. If you don't want to see him, you can hide out here. When no one answers your door he'll go away."

Stay here and miss seeing him? she nearly argued.

Okay, she'd gone crazy. She was pretty sure of it since she didn't know which was stronger: her dread at the idea of seeing him, or her overwhelming desire to be near him again.

"No, I have to go over there," she muttered as she watched Conor ring her doorbell.

It would have helped if he hadn't looked so good. Dressed in nothing better than jeans and a gray hoodie, he was still tall and broad-shouldered and all man, and even staring at him from that distance she was impacted by him. Much as she wished she wasn't.

She took a deep breath, sighed and stood up.

As she did Rachel said, "Do you want me to go with you? Or Jake could…"

Maicy laughed. "Conor isn't dangerous." At least

not beyond the effects he had on her. "It'll be okay. I'm sure he's here to formally say goodbye or something. I was just hoping not to do that. I should have known better. I'll call you tomorrow."

She went to her friend's front door but just as she opened it, Rachel said, "Maicy?"

She stopped, casting a questioning glance at her.

"I know you pretty well, right?" her friend said.

"Right."

"Then listen to me when I tell you that you really like this guy. Maybe what you felt for him died and now it's back. Maybe it never went away and you just buried it really, really deep. But the way you are about him is not the way you've been about anyone else. Not Drake. Not Gary. Nobody the whole time I've known you. It's a way I'm scared you'll never be about anyone else. So for once could you maybe try not being Tough-Maicy, let nature take its course just a little and see where it might be able to go from here with him?"

No. That was the answer to that question because if she let herself not be Tough-Maicy she wasn't sure how she would come out of this with her heart intact. So it was Tough-Maicy who was going across that street.

But that wasn't what she said to her friend.

"Sure," she lied.

Rachel gave her a small, sad smile that told Maicy she saw through her. But being a good friend, she didn't say that. She only nodded. "Yeah, call me…"

"Tomorrow," Maicy repeated before she went out the door and crossed the street.

Apparently Conor was on the alert because even with his back to her he sensed her approach and glanced over his shoulder.

When he recognized her he turned to face her. "There you are! Do I have the wrong house?"

"No, this is my place. I was at Rachel's."

"Ah, she's not only your best friend, she's your neighbor."

"Where did you get my address?" she asked as she unlocked her front door.

"Internet. Was it supposed to be a secret?"

He followed her inside and she closed the door behind them, thinking how strange it felt to have him there, in her house.

"No, it isn't supposed to be a secret. I guess I'm just wondering why you went to the trouble of finding it. Is everything okay? Is Declan all right? Your sister?"

"Declan is still in ICU but he's stable. Kinsey is fine but her future-mother-in-law has bronchitis and needed her. I gave her the green light to staying the night. The storm moved east, Maryland airports are closed now, so I'm here until they reopen and Kinsey and I can have a little time together later. Seemed like you and I just got cut off, though, and—"

He was rambling from one subject to another and he stopped himself to glance around at the living room she'd led him into.

"Nice place," he concluded. "Do you have renters upstairs?"

She recalled explaining her plans for the place when they'd talked about Gary. "Not yet. It still needs a few finishing touches before I can rent it. Gary was going to do them after the honeymoon. Now I'll have to hire someone…" Okay, maybe she was rambling slightly, too.

This was just weird. At the cabin, in Northbridge, even at the farmhouse, it had all seemed as if they were on more neutral territory. But this was *her* house. Where she lived her real life. Not only was he not a part of that, she'd been determined that once she got back to her real life, she'd leave her time with him behind.

Plus he looked so good there. So right. So much more like who she'd pictured sharing this house with than Gary ever had. And that was *not* an idea she could entertain!

She didn't invite him to sit but she perched stiffly on the arm of her white sofa and stared at him expectantly. It was not only an inquiry about why he'd come but also an attempt to convey the message that he shouldn't have.

But behind it she was drinking in the sight of that dark hair, that chiseled face, those sparkling cobalt blue eyes that she knew were going to haunt her forever.

"So if everything is all right…" she said to prompt him to tell her why he was there.

"Is that Rob kid in love with you or something? He wouldn't let me near you," he said, still not giving her a clue about this visit.

"He's a good kid. He looks out for Rachel like that, too. He and Jake had to kind of butt heads before Rob would get out of the way. He might be her little brother but he thinks of himself as her protector," she said, telling the truth but omitting the fact that she'd enlisted Rob's protectiveness.

"He thought he needed to look out for you with me?"

"He doesn't know you."

"And you didn't set him straight so we could say goodbye."

"Is that why you're here?" Maicy asked. "Because I didn't think we really needed to have some kind of big, dramatic farewell. I mean, I'm grateful that you followed me all the way from Northbridge and kept the car from stalling, but once we got here—"

"Yeah, I know, that was just gonna be it, we both needed to get on with our own stuff. But I realized that that's not going to do it for me."

Maicy raised her chin at him challengingly, not willing to drop her defenses.

Conor seemed to ignore it and went on to tell her what he was talking about, things he'd thought about earlier that evening, how he'd made his decision to resign his commission with the navy and do another residency to alter his medical specialty.

"I don't know for sure where we stand now, Maicy," he said once he'd spelled it all out for her. Then he amended it to, "I don't know where *you* stand. But I know what I want us to be. I loved you eighteen years ago—maybe you don't believe it, but I honestly did— and because I didn't do what you wanted me to do to prove it, I know I hurt you. I did harm—something I've devoted my life to *not* doing. I can never be sorry enough for that…"

He paused as if that carried so much weight it needed a moment of silence.

Then he said, "But out of what happened, you became the person you are now. And tonight, watching you walk away with that kid, knowing this time together was supposed to be the end… I knew I couldn't just let it happen. I love you, Maicy. I love who you are now more than that boy I was loved the girl you were…"

Another pause. Or maybe time stopped for a split second because that was how it seemed to Maicy as she tried to grasp what he was saying.

"So where I stand is where you stood eighteen years ago," he continued. "In front of you with a new plan for the future. One that has me becoming a civilian and doing a reboot of my career that'll make me a rookie again for a while. But one that could also—once I get Declan on his feet again—put me here, in Denver... with you, if you'll have me..."

Even without an invitation, he moved to perch on the arm of the white overstuffed chair that was at an angle to the couch. Closer to her now, he leaned forward and held out his hands in silent request for hers.

"Don't make me say goodbye to you...not now, not ever again," he said resolutely. "Let me...us...have what we thought we'd have—the rest of our lives together..."

Maicy didn't give him her hands. Instead she stared at his as so many things went through her mind, feeling as if something in her had split and left two halves at odds with each other—half that melted at the things he was saying, half that shied away from it the same way she'd shied away from Drake's proposal.

It was that latter half that was thinking that Conor was right when he said that she wasn't the girl he'd known years ago. And she never wanted to be that girl again—not in any way.

It was that half that *needed* to be strong and independent, to take care of herself because that was what made her feel secure and comfortable. She liked everything that she'd become once she'd risen from the ashes he'd left her in and she would not, under any circumstances, let go of her identity or agree to anything that ever threatened it. And to that half of her, the feelings for him that were fighting to take her over seemed like a great big, looming threat.

But yes, from that other half of her, those feelings for him *were* fighting fiercely to be set free. That half of her that had won out when she'd fallen asleep the night before. And it was begging her to take his hands now and jump at what he was suggesting.

But then what? she asked herself. Then did the soft half come out and stay out for good? The half that left her unprotected, that put her at risk? The kind of risk her mother had taken with her father over and over, getting hurt every time?

Conor wasn't her father, but he *had* let her down once before and devastated her in a way that was similar to what she'd watched her mother go through. It was why she'd convinced herself that she was better off with him out of her life. Was she really going to do what her mother had done and put herself in line for getting hurt again?

Not only didn't she take Conor's hands, she closed her own into fists that retreated from his.

But even as she did, that softer half of her told her that maybe she wasn't being completely fair.

Years before, Conor hadn't been on board with her plan, but it wasn't because he wanted to leave her. It was just that he'd wanted to stick to the original plan, to do what he'd thought was best for them both. He *hadn't* wanted them to break up.

Which, she guessed, made her actions more like her father's than Conor's actions had been because *she'd* been the one to jump ship when he hadn't given her what she'd wanted.

So was it possible that she *could* count on him? That he wouldn't disappoint her again?

She'd had to count on him at the cabin and he'd

come through for her at every turn there—he'd looked after her even in the middle of his own worries and fears and frustrations over his brother.

He hadn't let her down once they'd reached Northbridge, either, she admitted to herself. He'd stayed at the hospital, waited for her, done his best to get her the tests he'd thought she should have.

And afterward, he'd insisted on being by her side for the dance that could have turned into something embarrassing or painful—instead, his support had helped her through that awkward situation and made the whole thing better.

And she'd also been able to count on him helping her get back to Denver—another thing that he could have left her to deal with on her own.

When she honestly thought about it and factored in that it *hadn't* been Conor who had broken his commitment to her years ago, she also had to admit that there wasn't really any question about his loyalty or commitment to anything—to every plan he made, to his family, to everything he did. Even now, when he was dissatisfied with his choice of careers, he was dissatisfied because emergency medicine *didn't* allow him to make the kind of commitment he felt he needed to make to his patients. And as for the military, he'd decided on a course that would still leave him serving veterans and country in order for him to keep on honoring those commitments, just in a different way.

So was this all doubt and insecurity less about him and more about her?

She hadn't figured that out when he interrupted her confusion to say, "I'm not asking what that Drake guy asked of you. I want you to be who you are, I don't want you to change a thing about yourself or what you've built for yourself—I'm proud as hell of what you've accomplished, Maicy. I just want you to let me in so I can be a part of it, so you can be a part of where I'm headed from here."

He wanted her to let him in...

That had been one of Drake's accusations when she'd turned him down—that she wouldn't let him in, that she wouldn't let any man get too close. It was something Rachel thought, too.

But if she was completely honest with herself—which she was being at that moment—she had chosen to be with Drake and with Gary specifically because they weren't the kind of men who could convince her to fully open her heart. She hadn't had the kind of feelings for them that made her too vulnerable. The kind of feelings that had formed any real connection to them. The kind of feelings that had the ability to genuinely jar her when those relationships ended. Instead she'd had only safe, superficial feelings for them.

But is that really what you want? the Not-Tough-Maicy side asked in a voice that sounded a lot like Rachel's.

Safe, superficial feelings for men she could take or leave without any problem?

Not letting anyone get close enough to risk them hurting her?

Being so stubbornly independent and self-reliant that she really would end up dying alone?

But what was the alternative? Tough-Maicy argued. Risk being wiped out the way she had been eighteen years ago?

Because if she opened the door to what Conor wanted,

to what Conor was asking, if she opened the door to the kind of feelings she'd had during this last week and in his arms last night, and it didn't work out this time, it could be just as bad as it had been that other time...

She felt her head shaking no without consciously doing it herself, refusing Conor, refusing the softer side of herself and all the feelings, refusing to let him in...

"Maicy..." He said her name in a soothing voice. He leaned forward enough to put that handsome face in her line of vision.

And whether it was the beckoning tone or one look at him, it somehow altered her focus. It somehow made something in her settle slightly and think more clearly, more rationally.

Clearly and rationally enough to recognize that she couldn't ever again be where she'd been eighteen years ago.

Eighteen years ago she'd been barely more than a child. She hadn't had the ability for true independence, she hadn't had any resources.

But now she did have those things. And she also had the knowledge and the certainty that she could take care of herself, if she needed to. And Conor wasn't asking her to step away from her independence the way Drake had. Conor was honoring her accomplishments and showing a willingness to change his own course to accommodate them.

But he could still hurt her, she thought as she looked at that face that she never got enough of.

Losing him could hurt her really, really badly—it had already hurt just having him leave her behind at the repair shop despite the fact that she had orchestrated that.

"I am not going to let this be another ending for us," he said then, sharply enunciating each word. "Get that through whatever is going on in that head of yours and know this—we're together again because we're meant to be together, and I will do whatever I have to to get us there forever. To keep us there."

She didn't doubt that.

And slowly, little by little, looking into his eyes, those two halves of her began to merge into a whole that was somehow Tough-Maicy with softer edges— the person she was now with only a bit of the girl she'd once been.

And all of her was overflowing with feelings for Conor that she suddenly knew had taken her over regardless of how much she'd fought them.

She loved him. In spite of herself, maybe. Certainly in spite of their history. But she did love him. She couldn't deny it even when she tried to. And she knew she had to take the risk that brought with it.

She inhaled, held her breath, then exhaled, unclenching her fists but still not taking either of those big hands he had extended to her.

"You realize that I owe you a *no*. That you have it coming," she said.

He didn't take her seriously because he gave her a crooked, one-sided smile. "Go ahead, get it out of your system. I'll just keep asking until you think you've evened the score and we can move beyond it." The smile turned more engaging, more enticing. Sexier. "Or you could just be the bigger person and skip that part because you know you really do love me."

"Oh, do I?" she said.

The smile took another turn and became sweet and

boyishly charming. "I hope so. I came over here hoping so…" Then devilish. "You better not have just been using my body last night…"

Maicy laughed, thinking about that body of his. And how much she wanted it again right at that moment.

"Marry me, Maicy," he said then, quietly, earnestly, sincerely. "I love you more than you will ever know and I need you to be my wife."

"Or what?"

"Or the rest of my life will be just going through the motions."

He didn't merely leave his hands offered to her then, he took hers and held them firmly.

"Marry me," he repeated.

Her feelings for him were running rampant, and she was scared all over again by their strength and depth and bounds.

He really could hurt her…

But she also suddenly realized that she had to trust that he wouldn't. To trust him. Because she loved him too much to spend any more of her own life without him.

"Okay," she whispered.

He grinned. "Now tell me you love me as much as I love you," he instructed as if he knew she had to be talked through this.

"You know I do," she said in a low voice, as if it was hazardous to say it too loudly.

The grin melted into a smile that looked relieved. "I was counting on it but I need to hear it."

"I do love you, Conor," she said, still struggling through her own fears to admit it. Then she smiled and added, "Just ask Rachel."

"You told her what you wouldn't tell me?"

"No, she just knew."

He nodded sagely. "I don't care who knows as long as it's true," he said, standing and pulling her to her feet, too, so he could wrap his arms around her and hold her tight.

Those arms that she'd slept in last night and wondered how she was going to go on without.

Now she wouldn't have to...

She slipped her own arms under his and pressed her hands to his broad back as he bent down to kiss her.

And as she closed her eyes and gave herself over to that kiss, to him, to a future and forever with him, it slowly seeped in that she was finally where she truly belonged.

That whatever it had taken to get them there wasn't important anymore.

That all that mattered was that they'd rediscovered each other.

And that neither of them ever again let go.

* * * * *

Don't miss the first story in the
CAMDEN FAMILY SECRETS *miniseries*

THE MARINE MAKES HIS MATCH

Find more great reads at www.Harlequin.com

Get 2 Free Books,
Plus 2 Free Gifts —
just for trying the
Reader Service!

✦ **HARLEQUIN**®
SPECIAL EDITION

"Lydia Grant, assistant manager," he read, then lifted a questioning glance to her. "Is that you?"

Her head made a quick bob, causing several curls to plop onto her forehead. "That's me. Assistant manager is just one of my roles at the *Gazette*. I do everything around here. Including plumbing repair. You need a faucet installed?"

"Uh, no. I need a wife."

The announcement clearly took her aback. "I thought I misheard you earlier. I guess I didn't."

Enjoying the look of dismay on her face, he gave her a lopsided grin. "Nope. You didn't hear wrong. I want to advertise for a wife."

Rolling the pencil between her palms, she eyed him with open speculation.

"What's the matter?" she asked. "You can't get a wife the traditional way?"

As soon as Zach had made the decision to advertise for a bride, he'd expected to get this sort of reaction. He'd just not expected it from a complete stranger. And a woman, at that.

"Sometimes it's good to break from tradition. And I'm in a hurry."

Something like disgust flickered in her eyes before she dropped her gaze to the scratch pad in front of her. "I see. You're a man in a hurry. So give me your name, mailing address and phone number and I'll help you speed up this process."

She took down the basic information, then asked, "How do you want this worded? I suppose you do have requirements for your…bride?"

He drew up a nearby plastic chair and eased his long frame onto the seat. "Sure. I have a few. Where would you like to start?"

She looked up at him and chuckled as though she found their whole exchange ridiculous. Zach tried not to bristle. Maybe she didn't think any of this was serious. But sooner or later Lydia Grant, and every citizen in Rust Creek Falls, would learn he was very serious about his search for a wife.

Don't miss
THE MAVERICK'S BRIDE-TO-ORDER
by Stella Bagwell, available September 2017 wherever
Harlequin® Special Edition books and ebooks are sold.

www.Harlequin.com

LOVE
Harlequin
romance?

Join our Harlequin community to share your thoughts and connect with other romance readers!

Be the first to find out about promotions, news, and exclusive content!

Sign up for the Harlequin e-newsletter and download a free book from any series at

www.TryHarlequin.com

CONNECT WITH US AT:

Harlequin.com/Community

 Facebook.com/HarlequinBooks

Twitter.com/HarlequinBooks

Instagram.com/HarlequinBooks

Pinterest.com/HarlequinBooks

ReaderService.com

**ROMANCE WHEN
YOU NEED IT**

HSOCIAL2017

Reward the book lover in you!

Earn points from all your Harlequin book purchases from wherever you shop.

Turn your points into *FREE BOOKS* of your choice
OR
EXCLUSIVE GIFTS from your favorite authors or series.

Join for FREE today at
www.HarlequinMyRewards.com.

Harlequin My Rewards is a free program (no fees) without any commitments or obligations.

MYR17

THE WORLD IS BETTER WITH

Romance

Harlequin has everything from contemporary, passionate and heartwarming to suspenseful and inspirational stories.

Whatever your mood, we have a romance just for you!

Connect with us to find your next great read, special offers and more.

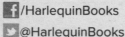

/HarlequinBooks

@HarlequinBooks

www.HarlequinBlog.com

www.Harlequin.com/Newsletters

HARLEQUIN®

A *Romance* FOR EVERY MOOD™

www.Harlequin.com